ST. MARTIN'S

MINOTAUR

MYSTERIES

Other titles from St. Martin's **Minotaur** Mysteries

St. Martin's Paperbacks is also proud to present
these mystery classics
by Ngaio Marsh

"HERE, SALLY . . . COME, SALLY . . ." SHE CALLED.

Sally answered vociferously, but remained where she was.

"She's got herself caught behind one of the machines! Mr. Arbuthnot will be furious!" Furious herself, Dora Stringer shoved Annabel to one side and barged through the door.

"Come out here, you filthy little beast! Where are—?"

The scream was so piercing and sudden that Annabel recoiled. It seemed to ricochet from every surface, freezing her in her tracks, momentarily cutting off all coherent thought, almost deafening her. Annabel blinked and tried to pull herself together.

. . . Annabel pushed past Dora Stringer expecting, at the very least, to see total devastation. . . . At first glance, everything seemed all right, the computers in place and undamaged, the work station in order.

"ARTHUR! ARTHUR!" The scream turned into a name. Dora Stringer hurled herself forward, falling on her knees beside a body lying on the carpet. "ARTHUR!"

THE
COMPANY
OF CATS

MARIAN BABSON

St. Martin's Paperbacks

Originally published in Great Britain by HarperCollins Publishers as *The Multiple Cat*.

THE COMPANY OF CATS

Copyright © 1999 by Marian Babson.
Excerpt from *To Catch a Cat* copyright © 2000 by Marian Babson.

Library of Congress Catalog Card Number: 98-52967

ISBN: 0-312-97501-5

Printed in the United States of America

St. Martin's Press hardcover edition / April 1999
St. Martin's Paperbacks edition / July 2000

10 9 8 7 6 5 4 3 2 1

1

Perhaps, if it hadn't been for that morning's flurry of bills cascading through the letter box, she would never have got involved. She stared unbelievingly at the telephone bill, midway between despair and fury. Couldn't that idiot who had rented her cottage pick up the telephone even once without dialling the International Exchange? Just look at the size of that bill!

Annabel Hinchby-Smythe closed her eyes, tossed back the remains of her martini and took a deep breath and then a deeper one.

Oh, the creature was probably honest enough and would pay the bill eventually. Meanwhile, however, she had to pay it herself or risk having the phone cut off—and he would expect to find it in working order when he returned from his trip to Italy.

Annabel frowned and absently poured herself another martini. It was just unfortunate that money was so tight at the moment. It seemed as though every company in her slim portfolio of stockholdings had issued a profits warning and notice of decreased dividends. The stock market appeared to be going through another of its periodic crises.

Furthermore, her lucrative little sideline of supplying items to the gossip columns appeared to have dried up. Either everyone had started behaving themselves, which was improbable, or they were lying exceptionally low. Also, most of her generation had sown their wild oats, reaped their whirlwinds and were now quietly breeding polo ponies in Argentina, raising sheep in Australia or—in one notorious case— writing poetry in a cloistered monastery.

Annabel drummed her fingers on her glass, setting the clear liquid rippling. Obviously, she needed to widen her circle of friends and acquaintances.

So it was just as well that she had agreed to attend that party being given by some highly dubious social climbers tonight. It was also fortunate that the opportunity to sublet her cottage had arisen at the same time that dear Dinah, who was taking a three-month cruise in the Far East to recover from the stress of recent events, had offered her the Cosgreave pied-à-terre in Knightsbridge. Lady Cosgreave could be benevolent— in her own way—or perhaps she considered it further assurance against Annabel's changing her mind about selling that very interesting story to the newspapers. So far, Dinah had done a sterling job at covering up the scandal.

Not that Annabel would dream of doing any such thing—and Dinah should have had more faith in her— but it *was* useful to have a rent-free Central London base while she collected rent on the short-term let of her own cottage.

That helped—quite a bit. Now, if only she could unearth a few juicy items to sell to the gossip columns . . . it had been so long since some of them had heard from her that they might be forgetting she existed—and that would never do.

The grandmother clock in the front hall chimed suddenly, startling her and reminding her that it was time to get changed for that cocktail party.

Initially, the party was disappointing. She had gleaned only one item she could sell on to a column and collected two leads to possibly developing stories she needed to keep an eye on. Nothing spectacular, though, nor even very interesting, just column-fillers for those dull days when nothing much was happening. On the other hand there seemed to be an awful lot of those days. She could not escape the feeling that the progeny of her own generation were a lot less enterprising, not to mention entertaining, than their parents and even grandparents had been.

It was borne in upon her gradually that a man on the fringe of her group was watching her intently and had been since she had been the centre of another group she had been regaling with a second—or perhaps even third-hand—anecdote about Sybil Colefax, the famous between-the-wars society hostess and interior designer. After the laughter had died down and the group broke up and re-formed, he had followed her to stand on the edge of her new group, watching and listening.

Absently, Annabel wondered if she had picked up a stalker and, if so, whether the information would be of any value—or interest—to one of the gossip columns.

As this group broke up, the man finally made eye contact with her and moved closer to speak to her.

"You're an interior designer, I gather," he said. "I heard you talking about it. I've been thinking about doing up my place lately, but I keep putting it off because I never quite knew who I ought to get to do it. I wonder if you'd be interested in taking on the job, er, assignment?"

"Ummmm . . ." Annabel went through the pantomime of reluctance, although it was the best offer she'd had in months. "Actually, I *am* rather busy just now . . ." She gave him an encouraging smile. How difficult could interior designing be? "But I might be able to squeeze in a preliminary consultation. Er, my rates are rather high, you realize?" She tilted her head so that her diamond earrings flashed at him.

"Of course." Gold glittered at his cuffs as he swept aside her demur. "They would be. Anyone who worked with Sybil Colefax . . ."

"Mmmm." How old did he think she was? His attitude was cheering, however. Numbers obviously meant little to him, whether in terms of money or years. She mentally doubled the amount she had thought of quoting; if he blanched, it could always be lowered.

He simply nodded, however, and handed her his card, then hesitated expectantly.

"Oh, I'm afraid I don't have my card with me," Annabel said haughtily. "This is a social occasion, after all." She raised an eyebrow in faint reproof. (It was all coming back to her—those few occasions when she had seen interior designers in action in the homes of her friends: the customer is always wrong.) "I wasn't expecting to do any business here."

"Of course, of course . . . I'm sorry." He was immediately cowed, contrite and apologetic—all the hallmarks of the perfect client.

"It *is* possible," she forgave him graciously, "that I might be able to fit you in between two other clients. One is off to Bermuda for six months, so there's no desperate urgency about her country house . . ."

"I'd be most grateful if you could," he said humbly. "I'm sure you know how it is. One drifts along for ages thinking vaguely 'I must do something about this place.' Then, suddenly, the opportunity presents itself and you can't wait to get it done."

"So many clients feel that way." The Opportunity smiled graciously, working herself deeper into the part with every passing moment, while calculating rapidly. She could get to the library first thing in the morning and take out a selection of books on interior design, bone up on them over lunch and get the patter—not that he was likely to know the difference.

"You'll want to inspect the flat. Let me—" He retrieved his card and scribbled something on the back of it. "This will get you in if I'm not there." He hesitated. "I'm afraid it's rather ghastly. I didn't realize how bad it was until Sally moved in—not that she's critical, she's too polite for that. But it's amazing the way you can tell what she's thinking."

"Women *are* more sensitive to their surroundings," Annabel agreed.

"All females are, I suppose." He looked faintly surprised. "I never thought of it that way before. Er . . . how soon do you think you might . . . ?"

"Perhaps I might find time to take a quick look tomorrow afternoon—lateish, of course, before I meet friends for dinner."

As soon as she got back to Lady Cosgreave's flat, she reached for the telephone and dialled one of her sources. There was no point in doing all this homework without making sure that it was going to be worth the effort.

"Arthur Arbuthnot?" Xanthippe's Diary responded enthusiastically. "The rumour is that Croesus is his middle name. You mean you've got something on *him?*"

"No," Annabel admitted regretfully, noting that it sounded as though it would be very worth her while to keep her eyes open while she went about her new business. "I, um, was thinking of entering a business arrangement with him and, since I'd never heard of the man, I thought I'd do a bit of checking. Make sure he's solvent . . . and honest . . . and all that."

"No worries on the first score. Otherwise, I suppose he's as honest as any billionaire—if that's saying much. He's a bit of a dark horse, our Arthur. Nothing much known about him, dull as ditchwater. So dull"— the voice brightened—"that there well could be something going on below the surface. You're sure you're not on to something?"

"Not really . . ." Annabel had a sudden doubt. Hadn't Arthur Arbuthnot said something about how shabby the place looked when seen through the eyes of the lady who had moved in? What lady? "Anyway," she added tantalizingly, "it's far too early to say."

"Remember," Xanthippe purred, "we'd pay *very* well."

"If I find anything, you'll be the first to know," Annabel promised.

2

The address was close to Regent's Park. Not, unfortunately, one of the lovely Nash Terraces, but one of the great Victorian mansion blocks set farther back from the park. Behind the wrought-iron-gate-protected glass-fronted door, the dark oak-panelled lobby was not exactly welcoming.

The man sitting behind the reception desk was even less so. He glared at her with such open hostility that she had to make an effort not to step back.

"I'm here to see Mr. Arbuthnot," Annabel said crisply, holding her ground. "I'm expected."

"Name?" It was a surly drawl. He knew who she was.

"Annabel Hinchby-Smythe." There was no point in antagonizing him, he might be useful in the future, however unlikely it might seem. She gave him a perfunctory smile.

"Top floor," he admitted grudgingly. "Lift over there."

As he pushed himself away from the desk to indicate the location of the lift, Annabel realized that he was in a wheelchair. One leg ended just above the knee. He could not be more than twenty-six.

So it was nothing personal then. He just hated the world. She couldn't blame him for that. Everyone did at some point in their lives. It was obvious that he had better reason than most.

The moment she was ushered into the dark gloomy hallway, Annabel knew that she was on to a winner. *Anything* anyone did to this dump would be an improvement.

Antlered skulls lined both sides of the long narrow corridor—which would not be so narrow if all those antlers were not branching out into the overhead space like perverted trees. Just clearing them out would work wonders and then a lick of paint and perhaps a few pictures would transform the hallway into a more cheerful place.

There was a new lightness in Annabel's step as she followed the tall thin woman, who had not yet spoken a word to her, around the corner into a further long corridor, as gloomy and antler-ridden as the first.

The woman disappeared abruptly through a doorway on one side, without a backward glance and giving no indication as to whether or not Annabel was expected to keep following. Annabel began to get the feeling that she was not exactly welcome here..

Since all the other doors along the hallway were firmly closed, Annabel followed her reluctant guide into a small office where a large mahogany desk was placed in front of a window, so that its occupant could face the hallway. If the door remained open—and, somehow, Annabel got the feeling that it was never quite closed—everyone coming and going could be noted.

"I don't know why Mr. Arbuthnot has bothered you," the Broomstick-in-a-skirt said pettishly. "There is nothing wrong with this flat the way it is. Is there, Wystan?"

For the first time, Annabel realized that someone else was in the room. He stood with his back to the window, his face in the shadows, and yet Annabel knew that he was looking at her. She stiffened as his gaze struck her like a jet of ice water and flowed down her body from face to feet. She felt that he was assessing her age, sex appeal and . . . possible child-bearing capacity.

"Now, now, nothing to worry about, Dora," he said soothingly. "The place could do with a bit of brightening up."

She had obviously been judged and found wanting, negligible or, worse, perfectly safe. Annabel's face froze. This Wystan might not know it, but he had come perilously close to making an enemy. And she wasn't that fond of the Broomstick, either.

"If Mr. Arbuthnot really feels the need to have something done," the woman said coldly, "we can get the painters in. Although I don't see why we should." She looked at the dingy grey-green walls with complacency. "Everything is fine just the way it is."

The woman was a dark silhouette against the light of the window, dominating the room. Behind her, shadows swooped and fluttered as a pigeon landed on the windowsill.

"Get out!" She whirled and struck the windowpane

a savage blow, sending the pigeon streaking off in terror. "Flying vermin!" she muttered. "Too much vermin around here already."

"My appointment is with Mr. Arbuthnot." Annabel used her highest cut-crystal tones; for emphasis, she moved her hand so that her diamonds sparkled in the light. "Perhaps you would be . . . good enough . . . to let him know that I have arrived."

"I'll take her in." Wystan, whoever he was, moved forward hastily, perhaps even nervously, as the Broomstick whirled to face back into the room, radiating fury and annoyance.

"Come along." Wystan stepped between them. "I know Arthur is looking forward to your visit, er, consultation." He grasped Annabel's elbow tentatively and led her from the office.

"You mustn't mind Dora," he murmured as soon as they were safely out of earshot. "She's worked here so long she almost thinks the place belongs to her. Old retainer and all that, you know how it is."

"Too tiresome." Annabel forced an understanding smile to mask her dislike. Wystan was obviously the sort who perched on the fence, swaying first to one side and then to the other, depending on who seemed to be winning at the time. She had met that type before. Often, in fact.

"Means no harm," he vouched improbably. The Broomstick would do all the harm she could—and delight in it, in the unlikely event that delight came within the scope of her vocabulary, not to mention her emotional range.

Wystan gave a perfunctory tap on the door at the

end of the hallway and swung it open. "Your decorator is here, Arthur," he announced.

This was a room she would not dare touch—nor would she be required to. Computer terminals hummed in every corner, flickering screens threw up and discarded images faster than the eye could focus on them, a constant procession of figures marched across other screens, a low-level susurration of irregular signals—probably a code, but quantum leaps beyond Morse—throbbed somewhere in the depths of all the high-tech apparatus.

The Heart of Empire, Annabel thought irreverently, but a business empire, overbearing, multinational and whispering of wealth beyond avarice. The diffident little Mr. Arbuthnot was obviously far far more important than she had ever imagined. No wonder Xanthippe was so interested.

"Oh, splendid, splendid." Arthur Arbuthnot rose and advanced, hand outstretched to greet her, but with the weight of empire still riding on his shoulders. "I'm sorry. I intended to meet you at the door but"—he waved his hand about with an apologetic grimace—"one gets so caught up in the daily grind that one loses track of time."

"Quite all right," Annabel cooed forgivingly, but she was not deceived. For a moment, before he began to speak, his face had been a cold robotic mask, as much a part of the machines as though he had been plugged into one of the electric outlets himself. Loss of humanity might be the price of being an emperor in the brave new electronic world.

"No, no, I should have . . ." Even now he could not

quite make the transition to the human, flesh-and-blood world; he was much more comfortable interacting with machines. He never made the wrong move there.

"No problem at all, Arthur," Wystan said soothingly. "Dora and I were there to let her in. No harm done. Not as though"—the soothing tone tilted over into one less comforting—"you'd pressed the wrong button on one of your computers and wiped out the Hang Seng Index."

"Thank you, Uncle Wystan." Arthur's voice was carefully neutral, but it was clear that he was displeased. There were some things one did not joke about. "I appreciate your looking after my guest for me."

"Be careful! Don't let her in!" the Broomstick shrieked suddenly from across the hall.

Annabel stiffened again. This was carrying antipathy too far. The woman must be mad. "I'm perfectly able to see that you won't want this room touched," she said coldly.

"Hah!" Arthur Arbuthnot made a sudden dive at her ankles and she barely repressed a scream. Were they all mad? And why hadn't she left a note telling someone where she was going? It could be days before she was missed and then no one would know where to begin looking for the body.

"Got her!" He straightened up triumphantly, clutching a squirming armload of dappled brown fur. "She knows this is the one room she isn't allowed into," he explained apologetically to Annabel. "Cats are full of static electricity—that's why they aren't allowed near ammunition dumps or any sensitive areas."

"Oh, yes, I see." Annabel could feel her eyes widening. She looked at the array of mysterious machines crowding the room, at the cat, at the rather weird Arthur Arbuthnot and mentally began formulating excuses about too much work to take on any more, or perhaps a sudden summons to fly to some distant part of the globe to the help of an existing client. Money wasn't everything.

"And then there are all those little hairs flying about." He gave the cat a friendly jiggle and it began purring. "They can wreak havoc with delicate machinery. This is the only room barred to her so, naturally, it's the one she's determined to get into. There are moments when she makes me feel like Bluebeard." He stepped forward, leading them out of the nerve centre of his empire, and closed the door firmly behind him. "Shall we adjourn to the parlour? We'll be more comfortable there."

"Of course." Annabel followed him along the corridor, noting that the route was carrying them well away from the office where the Broomstick lurked. A shadow moved uneasily behind that half-open door, as though perturbed that the action was moving out of range of her sphere of observation. Annabel decided that it would be a delight to redesign the Broomstick's office, turning her desk around so that she faced the window with her back to the door. Venetian blinds over the window and quaint old Victorian screens blocking the door might also be a good idea. Poor Arthur Arbuthnot! Did he occasionally long for the happy bygone days of Machiavelli, when leaders could employ blind secretaries and deaf-mute personal assistants to carry out their orders?

"In here." Mr. Arbuthnot swung open a door at the end of the corridor, ushering her into what once must have been a grand drawing room with a magnificent view over the treetops of Regent's Park. Pity about the view inside the room. Still, it cheered Annabel.

Safely away from the faintly sinister humming lair of Future World, her spirits were lifting and this helped even more. Never had she seen a place so badly in need of redecoration. It couldn't have been touched since the 1890s, although an Art-Deco cocktail cabinet and a couple of uncomfortable-looking chromium-and-leather chairs gave mute evidence of a desperate attempt at modernization sometime around the mid-1930s.

"Do sit down." Mr. Arbuthnot began to wave her towards one of the chromium monstrosities, then realized his mistake and indicated a Victorian gossip-bench instead.

Annabel perched on one seat of the S-shaped contraption and found herself almost cheek-to-jowl with Uncle Wystan, who had taken the other half of the perch. She hadn't realized he was still with them.

"Er . . ." Neither, apparently, had Mr. Arbuthnot. "Was there something you wanted to see me about, 'Uncle' Wystan?" This time, there could be no mistake: there was a certain ironic stress on the word "Uncle."

"Oh, um . . ." Uncle Wystan appeared rather confused, but gave the impression that this was a natural state with him. "I, er, just thought you might like me to sit in on the session, give the benefit of my advice, perhaps. Artistic strain runs in my family, you know. My Aunt Etta painted watercolours, exhibited in the Royal Academy Summer Show every year up to the war, when they put her in the Camouflage Corps." He sighed deeply. "Ruined her technique, blighted a promising career."

"I think I'll stick to professional advice." Mr. Arbuthnot spoke with elaborate patience. "If you don't mind, Uncle Wystan."

"Oh, certainly, certainly. Don't buy a dog and bark yourself, eh? Oh, sorry." He blinked at Annabel. "No offence intended."

"None taken," Annabel said graciously. Inwardly, she squirmed a bit. What if Mr. Arbuthnot ever found out the truth about her professionalism?

"That's settled then." Mr. Arbuthnot looked pointedly towards the door. In his arms, the cat narrowed her eyes at Uncle Wystan, her tail lashing menacingly.

"Oh, er . . ." Faced with their combined disapproval, Uncle Wystan twisted around and struggled to his feet. "I suppose I ought to go and find Zenia, although she told me—" He broke off unhappily, as though realizing that whatever he had been told was not for public consumption.

"*There* you are, Wystan!" The voice from the doorway cut across his discomfiture. If the glasses in the cocktail cabinet had been more fragile, it would have shattered them. The cat twitched her ears and emitted a protesting grumble.

"And there *you* are, Aunt Zenia." Mr. Arbuthnot

had no need to turn around, there was a resigned note in his voice.

Annabel had a clear view of the woman in the doorway; carefully, she kept her facial muscles motionless. "Uncle" Wystan was explained—and not as some late-arriving progeny of the Arbuthnot family. Aunt Zenia was of a suitable age to be an aunt to Arthur Arbuthnot, Wystan was clearly her superannuated toy boy, their union only slightly dignified by marriage. No wonder Wystan was younger than his "nephew". No wonder Mr. Arbuthnot got that strange note in his voice when he addressed his "uncle." In years gone past, and without an obliging woman to support him, Wystan would have been a remittance man.

"Hmmmph!" The woman had been observing Annabel as closely as Annabel had been observing her, but with considerably less subtlety. The slightly bulging brown eyes blinked and dismissed her, turning to Arthur Arbuthnot. She was nearly as thin as the Broomstick, but it was a carefully sculpted, expensively maintained thinness, set off by a suit from the latest fashionable designer. Annabel could not quite name the designer, but she was certain that the price would have been in the four figures; she was equally certain that Wystan had not been the one to pay for it.

"I'd like to speak to you, Arthur," Aunt Zenia said. "I do wish you'd put that cat outside—you know how flying fur reacts on me."

"You can always go back downstairs to your own quarters," Arthur said mildly. "Sally lives here and she can shed her fur anywhere she likes. This is her home."

"I must speak to you, Arthur!" An impatient hand waved away any more of his protests. "Perhaps Miss Thingee, here, can take the cat outside for a few minutes."

"It's Mrs. Hinchby-Smythe, actually." Annabel bared her teeth at the revolting woman.

"Really?" The note of surprised disbelief was obviously intended to be insulting—and succeeded. Even Uncle Wystan looked embarrassed.

"I do apologize for my family," Mr. Arbuthnot said quickly. The look he gave his aunt left no doubt about what would have happened to her had she not been family. Unfortunately, one can't fire one's aunt.

"Quite all right," Annabel said brightly. "There's no need to apologize for family—everyone understands that you're not responsible."

Zenia drew herself up but, before she could speak, her husband intervened hastily.

"Where's Neville? I thought he was supposed to be here today."

If he had been trying to change to a more pleasant subject, he had evidently chosen unwisely. Mr. Arbuthnot abruptly looked as though he had bitten into something sour.

"Are you expecting Cousin Neville, Aunt Zenia?" His voice was carefully controlled. "I thought he'd settled in Manchester."

"He still has his own room in my flat. He won't impinge on you in any way." Zenia was quickly on the defensive, Annabel noted. Was there, perhaps, some difficulty about her son? Possibly, even, a scandal?

If so, was it one Xanthippe might be interested in? Apart from the lure of extra cash for any juicy little snippets, Annabel would love to see Aunt Zenia in some sort of difficulty. She was already working up a strong dislike for the woman and would be prepared to bet that Zenia did not improve on further acquaintance.

In fact, there was no one in this flat she *did* like, apart from Arthur Arbuthnot and, possibly, his cat. The humans were a dead loss.

"What a beautiful cat." Annabel smiled at the complacent tabby lounging in Mr. Arbuthnot's arms.

"She is, isn't she? So beautiful she's made me take a new look at our surroundings." Mr. Arbuthnot stroked the cat's throat, eliciting a loud purr. "I decided her setting ought to be worthy of her."

Zenia had a nice line in snorts. She treated them to another.

Annabel choked back her own gurgle of amusement. So Arthur wanted his flat redecorated to set off not a woman he treasured but a cat.

"And I called her Sally," he continued, "because of the song. And because I found her in the alley, you see."

"Yes." Zenia's glittering eyes looked directly from the cat to Annabel. "As you may have noticed, Arthur has a *penchant* for alley cats."

3

"Here they are," a voice said from the doorway behind them. "We wondered where everyone was hiding."

A young man advanced languidly into the room— or perhaps his tight designer jeans would not allow him to move more quickly—followed by a slightly older woman, who was beautiful but had something about her which betrayed that alley cats were, indeed, endemic in this establishment.

"Neville, dear!" His mother greeted him warmly, pointedly ignoring his companion.

"Tara!" Wystan's enthusiasm made up for his wife's indifference. "Thought you were still in Mustique. Good to see you back. You're looking very— er . . ." A poisonous look from his wife stopped him dead. "Er, very tanned, very fit."

"Thank you." Tara moved past him dismissively, heading for the real object of her interest. "I brought you a little souvenir, Arthur." She extended a closed hand, turned it over and opened it suddenly. A sparkling fish on a string bounced in midair. "Actually, it's for Sally. What can one give to a man who has everything?"

A fond foolish smile spread over Mr. Arbuthnot's face as Sally stretched out a paw and swiped lazily at the dangling fish.

"She likes it," he said. "Thank you, Tara. Thank you very much." He took the toy from her and dangled it in front of Sally himself.

Zenia gave a sharp hiss of indrawn breath, glaring at Tara even more venomously than she had glared at her husband.

Interesting. Annabel made a mental note that the way to Mr. Arbuthnot's heart was clearly through his cat. And if it annoyed Zenia, so much the better. It was obviously a lesson Tara had already learned.

A flicker of movement beyond the doorway caught Annabel's eye. When she turned her head, no one was there. Yet she had the impression that someone had been hovering outside, eavesdropping.

The Broomstick, probably. Unable to utilize her observation post at this distance, she had left it and followed them to make sure she wasn't missing anything.

How did Arthur Arbuthnot put up with it? An overbearing secretary, a ghastly family, these depressing surroundings—or was he too engrossed in his business empire and his billions to notice much about his immediate environment? No wonder he was so fond of his cat.

On the other hand, he had begun to make a start on at least one thing that needed attention: this gloomy flat. She herself was scheduled to be the new broom to sweep this clean. Did he have further plans for some of his other problems? And what about the lovely Tara? Was she Neville's special friend or Arthur's? What sort of setup was this?

Definitely a promising one from the gossip point of view, Annabel decided. Judging from the undercurrents swirling around Wystan and Neville, there was a scandal or two in the background and, unless she missed her guess, quite probably another one waiting to happen.

First, however, her own status here had to be confirmed. With elaborate unobtrusiveness, Annabel glanced at her watch and then at Mr. Arbuthnot.

"Yes, quite." He caught the unspoken message. "I'll just finish showing you around and then you can send me your quotation."

A loud snort from Zenia expressed her opinion of this. Her nephew looked at her coldly. "Ah, yes, you wanted to speak to me, Aunt Zenia. Perhaps we could postpone it until—"

"I merely wanted to tell you that this whole project is ill-conceived and quite ridiculous. There is nothing wrong with this flat the way it is."

Annabel permitted herself a small wince and closed her eyes briefly. It was a reaction she had once observed in an official of an auction house when confronted with an inferior reproduction of a famous painting.

"Yes, quite," Mr. Arbuthnot agreed. "I think we're all well aware of your opinion by now, Aunt Zenia."

And it wasn't going to change a thing.

"Personally, I think you're right, Arthur." Tara weighed in on the winning side. "This place could do with a complete redesigning. It's too fusty for words."

"Not a bad idea, at all," Neville also plumped for the winning side, albeit with an uneasy sidelong glance towards his mother. "After all, if you didn't own the freehold, the terms of any lease would have insisted on your doing up the place every three years or so. It must be thirty-odd years since the old walls have seen so much as a lick of paint."

It was an unwise move. His cousin ignored him, but his family would deal with him later. Wystan gave a strangulated throat-clearing noise of warning. Tara moved a little farther away from him. His mother turned dangerously and glared at him.

"Come along," Mr. Arbuthnot said quickly. "This way." He led Annabel through a door at the other end of the room, safely away from the hostilities.

He led her through room after dreary room of the vast cavernous flat, each room more depressing than the last. They had been kept clean and dusted, but it was obvious that no one ever lived in them, or even visited them occasionally.

Annabel had never considered herself particularly sensitive to atmosphere but, by the time they wound up in a small study next to the computer room, she felt badly in need of a martini or three.

No such luck here, though. Instead, she took a deep breath and looked around the study. It could have been lifted directly from a gentlemen's club. Built-in bookcases, leather armchairs, lamps and side tables with the morning newspapers and the week's run of

the *Financial Times*. There was even a marble fire-
place with a fire laid in it waiting to be lit. It was the
most comfortable room in the flat and it was clear that
Arthur Arbuthnot spent most of his time here when
he wasn't working in the computer room.

"Well . . ." Mr. Arbuthnot motioned her to an armchair, slumped into the armchair opposite and looked
at her quizzically. "You begin to see the size of the
problem?"

She had the feeling that he was not referring solely
to the outdated apartment. This feeling was reinforced
when he asked anxiously:

"Are you willing to take it on?"

"Mmmm . . ." The hesitation was not entirely a bargaining ploy. When the offer was first made to her,
she had not yet encountered the Broomstick and Aunt
Zenia. Would the possible benefits be enough to
counterbalance the aggravations? "I'll think it over
and send you my quotation and then you can think it
over."

"That won't be necessary," he said quickly. "I've
already decided you're the designer I want. I simply
said that to keep Aunt Zenia quiet."

"Now that you mention it—" She decided to take
the bull by the horns. "I'd have to be assured that
there would be no outside interference in my work."

"You'll have a completely free hand. Any problems
and you just come straight to me."

"Well . . ." And, thinking of horns. "For one thing,
those revolting skull-and-antlers will have to go."

"I knew you were the right choice," he beamed.
Even the cat seemed happy about it. "Let me give you

a retainer right now. You can have the tradesmen send bills direct to me as they're incurred. Here, hold Sally for a minute." He stood up and thrust the cat at her.

Briefly, Annabel and the cat were nose-to-nose, blinking at each other. Then Annabel reached out and lowered the cat to her lap where it stood irresolute for a moment, then settled cautiously.

Distracted by the cat, Annabel did not see exactly what Mr. Arbuthnot did next. When she looked up, the slanted end section of the window enclosure had swung aside revealing a deep, shelved compartment into which he was reaching.

The cat watched intently, then stirred restlessly. Annabel tightened her hold and tried not to gasp. The shelves were packed solid with sheaves of international currency. If this was Mr. Arbuthnot's petty cash, it was enough to stock a Bureau de Change for a lesser man.

"Stay there, Sally," Mr. Arbuthnot said. "You've seen it all before." In a swift motion, he closed the safe and moved back to Annabel. "Sally knows all my secrets. She's the only one in this building I can trust."

"Ummm . . ." Annabel was mesmerized by the sheaf of banknotes in his hand. He couldn't intend to give all that to her . . . ?

"I hope this will do for your retainer." He extended it tantalizingly, then drew it back slightly. "You understand"—a crisp commanding note sounded in his voice—"I expect you to make other arrangements for any work you have on hand and begin here immediately."

He looked at her with utter confidence, in no doubt that she would comply. He was obviously well aware of the overpowering effect of the sight of a large amount of cash and had used that fact to his advantage in the past. One of the reasons, no doubt, that he kept large amounts of cash on hand. It had not escaped Annabel's attention that there was still a great deal of English money remaining in the secret safe, as well as all the foreign currency. It must be nice to be able to take off for foreign parts when one wished without the need to bother visiting a bank.

"That's all right, isn't it?" Her silence appeared to unnerve him, he glanced irresolutely at the stack of banknotes. "I realize that my family might make you think twice but, I assure you, they spend most of their time in their own quarters downstairs. If you'd like more money—?"

Danger money. The thought came to Annabel unbidden, startling her. *Aggravation money,* she amended. Aunt Zenia might be irritating and insulting, but it was overreacting to think of her as dangerous. As to the Broomstick . . .

"That will do—for now." Annabel stopped him as he turned back towards the window. It was flattering to think that he trusted her more than he did his family, but she felt that she would rather not watch as he opened the safe again.

"Good." He turned back and extended the money towards her. The cat stretched out her neck to sniff at it, then drew back disdainfully. *All right for some!*

As offhandedly as possible, Annabel accepted the money and tucked it into her handbag, while appearing to pay more attention to the cat who was settling back on her lap. She wondered if she were fooling anyone.

"Sally likes you." Arthur Arbuthnot sounded as though that was important to him.

"And I like her." Annabel picked up her cue. "She's a little darling, isn't she?"

"Indeed, she is," he said warmly. "I shall never know what she was doing starving in that alley. Except," he added thoughtfully, "that anyone can hit a bad patch in their lives."

"They certainly can," Annabel agreed fervently. Heaven knew she had hit more than enough bad patches in her own life. It had been difficult enough to have been born into the fringes of an aristocratic family with a bloodline good enough to get her presented at court, but without enough financial backing to fully finance her Season. Not that that mattered too much, times were already changing. Then she had met Young Hinchby—that first wild spring love, trailing in its wake the thrill of the engagement, the dream wedding and the happy-ever-after that had been blown to bits along with Young Hinchby in the skies over Korea while he was serving the last few months of his National Service. Good old Smythe had come along later, a lot later, bringing a quieter more mature love, but with a lot of laughter.

She glanced fondly at the twin diamonds on her left hand, smaller than Hinchby's diamond, but gleaming as brightly and also accompanied by a half-hoop diamond wedding band (Smythe was not to be outdone). They had found their dream cottage and settled in happily before a new photographic assignment had sent him to cover a small revolution in some obscure South American banana republic where he had aimed his camera at the wrong army at the wrong time. And that had been the end of Smythe and of another happy-ever-after. Men and their wars! Annabel had had as much as she could stand of both of both of them. She could not face that pain again, not that—at her present age—she was likely to be invited to. Yes, she had known bad patches with a vengeance.

Things were looking up again now, however. This interior-designing lark was a breeze—and Mr. Arbuthnot *had* said that that delightfully thick wad of banknotes now reposing in her handbag was just the retainer, hadn't he? She stroked Sally enthusiastically and was rewarded with a throaty purr.

A sharp buzz startled Annabel. Mr. Arbuthnot bent towards what had seemed to be a cigarette box on a nearby table and pushed a concealed button.

"Yes?" he snapped.

"Rio de Janeiro has just logged on." The high resentful voice of the Broomstick filled the room. "Your conference call can go through in five minutes. As scheduled."

"Thank you, Miss Stringer. Is Luther here yet?"

"Not yet. He hasn't reported in all day. And he knows how important this is. It's *too* bad of him." For a Broomstick, she had a whine of vacuum-cleaner intensity.

"He'll be here. You just take care of your end of things." Mr. Arbuthnot clicked down his switch, cutting off any further protests she might have made.

"You're very busy. I should leave now." Annabel gave Sally a little push, but the cat remained solidly entrenched on her lap.

"I'll take her." Mr. Arbuthnot picked Sally up. Annabel's skirt rose with her as Sally dug her claws into the material, indignant at being disturbed.

"Sorry. Let me—" Together they disentangled the claws and Annabel stood.

"I'll be round tomorrow, if that's convenient," Annabel said. "I'll bring some colour charts and swatches . . . and perhaps do a few preliminary sketches." She hoped that sounded sufficiently businesslike.

"Not too early," Mr. Arbuthnot said. "I'll be working late tonight. Perhaps eleven o'clock." -

"Fine." Annabel managed a smile, disguising the fact that she considered eleven practically the crack of dawn. She brushed at the cat hairs on her skirt, making a mental note to wear trousers, preferably brown, for the duration of this escapade.

Mr. Arbuthnot opened the door for her and she nearly collided with a young man just outside, standing so close to the door that he might have been just about to enter . . . or eavesdropping.

"Mrs. Hinchby-Symthe has agreed to take on the project, Luther. She begins tomorrow. You'll be seeing a lot of her and you're to give her every assistance. Mrs. Hinchby-Smythe, Luther is my personal assistant. If you have any problems and I'm not around, bring them to Luther. He'll deal with them."

Annabel shook hands perfunctorily with the earnest bespectacled young man as they murmured polite insincerities at each other. Behind the thick glasses, his glittering eyes told her that he was no more delighted to meet her than she was to meet him, that she was one more unwanted complication in a busy schedule and that the flat could stay the way it was for ever so far as he was concerned.

Another Broomstick. Only the gender was different. How did Mr. Arbuthnot manage to collect them all? Of course, they were both probably very efficient at their jobs—and Mr. Arbuthnot was so deeply involved with machines that he might not even have noticed any lack of human warmth in his associates, or perhaps he was more comfortable with them being that way. His family obviously provided more than enough emotion for his taste.

"We'll see you in the morning." Mr. Arbuthnot dropped Sally gently to the floor and went into his office.

"We'll coordinate"—Luther paused to assert his own authority—"on details then. I'll need a clear idea of when you plan to move the workmen in." With a curt nod, he followed Mr. Arbuthnot into the office.

Workmen? Annabel walked slowly down the corridor, so abstracted that she failed to notice Sally close on her heels. Overhead, the antlered skulls seemed to loom menacingly. Perhaps there was more to this interior-decoration business than she had thought. Now that Luther had brought up the subject of workmen, it was obvious that Annabel could not be expected to do everything by herself. Even taking down and disposing of the antlers would be a major project.

As for painting walls, hanging wallpaper, putting up curtains and all the rest of it . . .

For a start, she should have counted those sets of antlers. Annabel halted and turned to look back down the corridor. At the far end, something fluttered and stepped back. She was being watched. Again.

Get used to it, Annabel. It was obviously going to be one of the unwritten Conditions of Employment. Annabel's eyes narrowed. There must be a way of taking care of that.

Something brushed against her ankles and she looked down. "Sally!" She stooped and stroked the soft fur. "What do you think you're doing?"

"She thinks she's going to go out." Neville appeared behind her and swooped on the cat. "It's a good thing you noticed her. Cousin Arthur would have been very upset if Sally followed you outside and got lost." Something in his voice suggested that no one else would have been deeply concerned.

An almost palpable sensation of disappointment eddied down the corridor. It was enough to make Annabel wonder momentarily whether the place could be haunted. Then she realized the emotion had emanated from the Broomstick, who had been watching their progress with malicious glee, hoping that Annabel would get into trouble.

"I'll be more careful in the future," Annabel promised, loudly enough to further disappoint the Broomstick. She wouldn't be caught that way again, but she wondered how many other little traps might be lurking for her to fall into. She smiled graciously at Neville and Sally and closed the door thoughtfully behind her.

Downstairs, the entrance hall was deserted, the commissionaire no longer at his post. Or did he only man it when visitors were expected? Neville had betrayed the fact that Arthur Arbuthnot owned the entire building and Annabel was beginning to suspect that the young man in the wheelchair was just a gesture towards the pretence that this was an ordinary block of flats.

Still more thoughtfully, she closed the outer door and turned in the direction of Marylebone High Street, walking more quickly as her spirits lifted at the thought of the large amount of cash in her possession.

Time to do some shopping. She'd pick up an armload of decorating magazines, a bottle of gin and treat herself to a taxi back to Knightsbridge. Tonight she'd do her homework with the magazines and a bit of thinking. In the morning, she'd deposit the money in her bank account and then start work on the apartment.

4

After all that, the audience with a preoccupied Arthur Arbuthnot in the late morning was short and unsatisfactory. He seemed to have too many things on his mind to bother about making mundane decisions about colour schemes. Annabel was soon ushered out into the drawing room and left to her own devices, which meant beginning work—or appearing to.

She was amused to find that Sally had obviously appointed herself supervisor. The cat followed Annabel from room to room, sitting down and watching with great interest as Annabel wielded tape measure and notebook. With growing amusement, Annabel joined in the game, taking Sally at her own valuation.

"Would madam like the brocade or the velvet for the drapes?" Playfully, she dangled a swatch of each in front of the cat, who swatted at the rippling velvet.

"Oh, an excellent choice, madam—"

"You'll take your instructions from Mr. Arbuthnot—and no one else!" The Broomstick appeared in the doorway behind them, quivering with indignation.

She looked around, ready to do battle with the usurper. "Where did she go?"

"Who?" Annabel widened her eyes with exaggerated innocence. "I was just talking to the cat."

"The cat?" Still deeply suspicious, the Broomstick turned her head from side to side, peering into the farthest corners of the room before dropping her gaze to floor level where Sally sat looking up at her. "Do you mean to tell me you were using that tone having a conversation with that—that creature?"

I'd rather have a conversation with her than with you, Annabel thought. And it was not just because of the antipathy between them. She glanced down and met Sally's eyes, the unspoken agreement in them startled her. There could be no doubt that she and Sally were in perfect accord: the Broomstick was a Grade-A unmitigated pain in the—

"Were you looking for me?" a voice cooed from behind the Broomstick. Annabel suddenly realized who she had been suspected of consulting. Interesting. Was the Broomstick afraid that Tara was going to be in charge of things here in the very near future? And where did that leave Neville, who had appeared to be Tara's . . . um . . . escort, if nothing closer?

"I knew you were around somewhere." The Broomstick did not bother to conceal her hostility. Again, an interesting point. Either she was so secure in her job (*she knows where the bodies are buried* was the phrase that sprang to mind) or Tara was not yet in any position to be a threat.

"And now you've found me," Tara said smoothly. "There is a message from Mr. Arbuthnot." If looks

had any power at all, Tara would have shrivelled up
and become a heap of smouldering ashes on the carpet. "*He* will be 'delighted' to meet you in the downstairs lobby at twelve-thirty. I've made a reservation
at Rules for one o'clock."

"How kind of you," Tara cooed.

The temperature had dropped at least ten degrees.
Annabel looked at Sally with envy. Sally had retreated
under the nearest chair, curled up and gone to sleep.
Oh, lucky Sally. Unfortunately, Annabel couldn't do
that, but she could do the next best thing.

"Excuse me—" She replaced her tape measure,
swatches and notebook in her carrier bag and shouldered her way between the two quietly glowering
women into the comparative freedom and open space
of the long narrow corridor.

Pausing only to detach the smallest of the antlered
skulls, Annabel rammed it awkwardly into her bag.
Of course, it didn't fit. The long narrow skull slid into
the bag, but most of the antlers reared out of it and
the points nearest the skull bulged against the plastic,
threatening to rip it apart.

No matter, it would have to do. She had a luncheon
appointment of her own to keep and the antlered skull
was vital to her plans. *Sprat to catch a mackerel*, Annabel told herself, stalking through the downstairs
lobby and throwing the hovering young commissionaire a glare so challenging that he immediately found
himself something to do behind the reception desk.

Mackerel . . . a very artistic mackerel. A late last
night, faintly frantic telephone call to her American

artist friend, back in the village where they both lived, had produced the lead.

Annabel had hoped that Leonora Rice might be able to join her in doing up Mr. Arbuthnot's apartment—after all, paint was paint, wasn't it? But she had caught Leonora on the eve of her departure to set up her own exhibition in San Francisco and the best she had been offered was a substitute.

"So you're doing up the Arbuthnot apartment," Leonora had said, with a strange note in her voice. There had been a long reflective pause. "In that case, you might try Kelda. She'd be ideal—if she'd do it."

"Why shouldn't she?" Annabel asked.

"Oh . . . artistic temperament . . ." There was definitely a false, perhaps even evasive, tone there.

"Well, you know her better than I do," Annabel conceded. "In fact, I don't know her at all. What makes you think she'd be so right for the job?"

"Oh, she would." Leonora's voice firmed as she began to list her friend's qualifications. "She supports her own painting by freelancing. She does a lot of set-designing for theatre and TV, so she knows all sorts of odd places to find interesting fabrics and furnishings. Furthermore, she's in her Georgia O'Keeffe phase right now—and skulls are hard to come by in London, so you've got a great bargaining point. If you promise her all those antlers, along with some cash, she ought to be tempted enough to take the job on, even though—" Leonora broke off. "Or perhaps especially because—" She stopped again.

"She can have every last crumbling antler," Annabel promised, scribbling rapidly in her notebook. "Just tell me—Kelda who?"

"Just Kelda. That's all she uses. After all, you don't say Picasso who—or who Picasso—do you?"

"Actually," Annabel admitted, "I've never had occasion to say Picasso at all. Does she have a telephone number?"

"Of course . . ." Leonora hesitated. "But give me time to talk to her first before you call her. I'll make her see sense about this. It could work out so well—for both of you."

If she hadn't been distracted by pouring herself another martini, Annabel might have questioned the odd comments. As it was, she had written down the number and wished Leonora every success with her exhibition. Later, she had chanced her luck with the unknown Kelda, who had agreed to a discussion over lunch. She was on her way to that luncheon now.

It was love at first sight. Kelda and the antlers, that was. Annabel began to feel distinctly *de trop* as Kelda took the skull into her arms, crooned over it, stroked its antlers and generally made an exhibition of herself. Annabel shrank back in her chair—most unusually for her—and thanked her stars that they had met in such an out of the way watering hole. No one she knew was likely to venture into this place and witness her predicament. She hoped.

"How many more of these did you say there were?" Kelda suddenly switched from rapture to business. Her eyes were unnervingly shrewd within their kohl linings.

"Twenty-nine," Annabel said grimly. "The ancestral swine must have shot a whole herd of deer in his time—and those were just the trophies he kept."

"Thirty . . ." Kelda gloated. "And you're sure no one will object to my taking them away and . . . recycling them?"

"Play your cards right and they may even pay you to take them away. Just a joke," Annabel added hastily as Kelda's eyes gleamed. "And some of those skulls may not be in the best condition," honesty compelled her to admit. "They're pretty old."

"Doesn't matter." Kelda waved away the caveat. "Plenty can be done, even with fragments. My sister is a florist, she can gild them and use them in flower arrangements. The really good pieces I can incorporate into my organic sculptures and the in-between stuff can be used as props and for stage settings."

"You *are* ingenious." Annabel began to see why Leonora had recommended Kelda so highly. "And what do you feel about perhaps doing a bit of painting? Ordinary wall painting, that is."

"Nothing easier," Kelda said. "There are always a lot of kids hanging around the theatre ready to be helpful. I can round up a couple of them and have them wherever you want them. Of course, they may not be able to work *every* day . . ."

"What English workman does?" Annabel sighed, but her spirits were rising. As she had suspected, this interior-decorating business was a breeze. You just had to get your team in place and they'd do all the work while you swanked around and gave orders. "Er, you *will* be coming along, too?"

"Don't worry. I intend to stand over them while they take down those skulls. I wouldn't want anything to happen to them."

Annabel would have said that it was a century too late to worry about that, but smiled instead and nodded understandingly. There was no accounting for taste and Kelda had gone back to lovingly stroking the skull again.

Annabel averted her eyes and concentrated on her avocado, chicken and salad sandwich. "Arthur Arbuthnot won't know the place by the time we get through with it," she murmured optimistically.

"Arbuthnot?" Kelda raised her head and looked at her sharply.

"That's right. He's some sort of millionaire tycoon, I understand." Something about the unnatural stillness in Kelda's face rang a warning bell. "Do you know him?"

"I know . . . of him," Kelda said carefully. "He lives over by Regent's Park, doesn't he?"

"That's the one," Annabel said, quite as though there might be several to choose from.

Kelda remained silent for so long that Annabel began to feel the stirrings of panic. Was the girl changing her mind? Had she encountered Arthur Arbuthnot (a dark horse, if there ever was one) before—possibly around the theatre—and not enjoyed the encounter? What was wrong here?

"Are you all right?" Annabel asked.

"Oh, yes." Kelda pulled herself together with a visible effort. "Yes, I'm fine. I was just thinking . . ."

"And you're still game?" Annabel pressed anxiously. "You're going to take this on and continue in an . . . um . . . advisory capacity?"

"Oh, don't worry about that." Kelda's eyes flashed with a sudden unnerving avarice. "Who knows what else they might be throwing out? There are all sorts of possibilities. I wouldn't miss it for the world!"

When she saw the look on the Broomstick's face the next morning, Annabel decided that it had been worth all the hassle. Quivering with outrage, the Broomstick glared at the motley crew cluttering up the hallway she apparently regarded as her own and emitted several choking noises before she finally found her voice.

"What do you think you're doing?"

"Taking these down," Kelda answered from the top of the stepladder where she was carefully detaching a skull-and-antlers from the wall, a task she judged too delicate to allow anyone else to do.

"Stop it! Stop it immediately!"

Sally had been poised on her hind legs, one paw on the bottom step of the ladder. She looked from Kelda to the Broomstick and appeared to be rethinking her position.

"Get down! Get down at once!" The Broomstick stretched out both hands, threatening to shake the stepladder and dislodge everyone and everyone on it. Kelda shifted slightly and one foot swung loose; if she fell, she was going to kick out and ensure that someone's teeth came with her.

Sally prudently withdrew behind Annabel's ankles to watch future proceedings from that safe haven. Annabel backed up slightly, nudging Sally along with her.

"Get down, I said! At once!"

"Don't touch this ladder!" Kelda warned.

"What's going on here, Miss Stringer?" Arthur Arbuthnot appeared suddenly and Sally abandoned Annabel's ankles and ran to him. He stooped and picked her up with a soothing murmur, then his face froze as he turned to the humans. "Is there some problem?"

"These people are tearing the place apart!" Dora Stringer turned to him accusingly. "And just when you have all those important people arriving this afternoon."

"Nothing to do with us." Kelda clutched the skull protectively. She and Arthur Arbuthnot looked at each other briefly with mutual indifference. If they had ever seen each other before, they were consummate actors. "You just go away and get on with it."

"The effrontery!" Dora Stringer gasped, appealing to Arthur Arbuthnot. "Did you hear the way she spoke to me?"

"Mr. Arbuthnot—" Annabel decided it was time to take a hand. "I was under the impression that you had promised me there would be no interference from your staff."

"Quite right. So I did." Mr. Arbuthnot frowned at his secretary. "And I meant it. I'm sorry you've been troubled. It won't happen again—will it, Miss Stringer? . . . Miss Stringer?"

"As you wish." Dora Stringer abandoned her attempt to stare him down and turned away with an offended flounce. "But on your head be it!"

Annabel arched an eyebrow at the departing back. Why on earth was the woman taking it so personally? One would think she had shot every last damned deer herself.

"I'm sorry about that." Mr. Arbuthnot was staring after Miss Stringer with an expression that boded no good for her. "I'll see to it that it doesn't happen again." He followed Miss Stringer down the corridor with a purposeful step.

"Well! What was that all about?" Kelda waited until the pair were out of earshot before speaking. "Whose toes are we trampling on here, anyway? And why?"

"Good questions." Annabel shrugged, again feeling the uneasy tingling at the back of her neck that suggested that other prying eyes were watching. This was no time to give Kelda any answers—not that she had any.

"Who knows? Let's get on with the work." Annabel signalled to Peter and Paul, the teenagers who had appeared with Kelda and been introduced as her assistants—although a certain facial resemblance gave reason to suspect that they were actually relatives, perhaps cousins. One of them stepped forward to receive the skull and lower it reverently to the floor while Kelda moved on to detach the next in line from the wall.

They worked well; she had to give them that. By the end of the afternoon there was a respectable (so to speak) pile of skulls in one corner, which Sally was ecstatically investigating.

Numbers of unknown and unidentified people had

come and gone as they worked. Mr. Arbuthnot was obviously not the semi-recluse she had imagined. It was interesting to notice that very few of the visitors looked happy as they came away from their audiences with the great man.

Something was obviously going on. Whether it might make an item for the gossip column or the financial pages was yet to be determined. *Eyes and ears open, Annabel*, she told herself cheerfully. This job might be a nice little earner in more ways than one.

Meanwhile, she surveyed the now-denuded hallway with satisfaction. It looked twice as large already. Even the discoloured patches where the skulls had been removed were less obtrusive than the spreading antlers.

"We'll wash down those walls tomorrow," Peter, or perhaps it was Paul, assured her. "Get them nice and clean, a couple of days to dry out and then you can tell us what colour you want them."

"Excellent!" Annabel beamed on them.

Kelda, secure in her ownership of all the antlered skulls, beamed back. The boys nodded, unsmiling, but seemingly quite happy in the knowledge of a job well done and more to come in the morning. And, even better, payment at the end of the week.

Kelda piled their arms with the skulls and led them out of the apartment; she carried the largest and finest herself and was almost hidden behind her booty. It was to be hoped that she could see where she was going through the occasional gap.

Annabel lingered behind, half hoping to encounter Mr. Arbuthnot again. There were decisions he was going to have to make or, at least, be given the opportunity to make, although she suspected that fabrics and colour schemes were the least of his interests. But the gloomy apartment was silent, no whisper of life from any of its darkened rooms. All the earlier traffic had long since disappeared. Even the cat had vanished. She knew that she could not possibly be alone in the building, but there was nothing to prove she wasn't.

Except . . . that feeling of being watched by unseen eyes was back again. Hostile eyes.

Annabel swung around abruptly. No one there, of course. They were too fast—or too clever, watching from some secret vantage point. Perhaps one of those portraits so beloved in early films where, after the heroine had tiptoed trustingly down the hallway, the camera zoomed to a close-up of the portrait on the wall and the eyes blinked.

But there had never been a portrait in this hallway, only the endless antlered skulls. No human eyes could have hidden behind those curving empty eye sockets, nor was there a secret corridor running parallel with this one where a human body could lurk unseen. The grimy walls and innocent triangular patches were harmless. The menace emanated from some other source.

Annabel shivered and concentrated on practical matters. Pale lemon, she decided firmly. She would show Mr. Arbuthnot various colour charts of off-whites and yellows, but she would guide him to pale lemon. Then the more traditional brass wall sconces interspersed with some cheerful watercolours would complete the transformation.

She could see it all in her mind's eye and, satisfied, turned to the challenge of the living rooms. Not that it appeared that anyone had done any living in them for generations. Some of the pieces of furniture were quite acceptable, however, and should be retained. The gossip-bench, for instance, although it could do with reupholstering in a better material. That was something else she would have to get Kelda to organize: swatches of material, wallpaper books, all that sort of thing.

Annabel looked around irresolutely. The apartment still seemed utterly deserted, no gleam of light showed from any of the closed doors along the business end of the flat. It was quite possible that everyone had gone somewhere else; she had already realized that there were several exits from the penthouse, some of the short flights of stairs leading directly into the private quarters below, which she had not yet had a chance to investigate and, given that Aunt Zenia was living there, she was unlikely to have the chance to investigate.

Oh, well . . . she pulled herself together. What was she standing around here for? It was not as though she were a guest leaving a party to which she had been invited and wishing to say a proper goodbye and thank you to her host. She was one of the hired help now and her comings and goings were of no concern to her employer . . . so long as she did her job.

*   *   *

She was crossing the lobby when someone shouted at her. She drew herself up and swung around to see the commissionaire waving her over. She glared at him for a split second before remembering that the man, although young, was not able-bodied. She could go over to him much more easily than he could come to her.

"Here—" He spoke between gritted teeth, obviously having noticed her initial reaction and interpreted it correctly. He did not want pity, nor to have others make allowances for him, but it was the situation he was trapped in for the rest of his life. He was finding it hard to learn to live with it.

"Here!" He almost threw the small heavy envelope at her. "Arbuthnot left the keys for you. So you don't have to wait for anyone to open the doors."

"Thank you." So it had not escaped Mr. Arbuthnot's notice that Annabel had been forced to ring the apartment doorbell four times that morning before the Broomstick deigned to answer it. The envelope was very heavy, with more than one key in it.

"The big one is for the street door," he said, somewhat defensively. "I can't always be here to let people in."

"Of course not," Annabel agreed.

It was so much noisier down here at ground level that Annabel realized the penthouse must be soundproofed. The street noises outside were loud and harsh, the roar of a motorcycle almost deafening as it pulled up outside and a helmeted messenger got off and approached the front door.

Although she was expecting it, the loud shrill of

the bell made Annabel jump. Then there was silence. Across the wide expanse of lobby and through the grille on the door, the helmeted messenger and the young man in the wheelchair seemed to lock gazes. After a long moment, the messenger rang the bell again.

No one seemed in a hurry to open doors around here. Annabel wondered whether it were a matter of general policy or just bloody-mindedness on the part of the doorkeepers.

Just as the messenger raised his hand to ring again, the buzzer sounded sharply, releasing the door catch. The messenger took swift advantage, pushing the door open before it could relock, then hesitated, seemingly not anxious to approach the desk. He removed his helmet, suddenly looking young and vulnerable. Again his gaze crossed with that of the young man in the wheelchair; they were about the same age. He hesitated a moment longer, then moved forward slowly.

"Wotcher, Mark," he said uneasily. "You all right, mate?"

"Never been better," Mark sneered, rolling back from the desk so that his stump could be seen. The unfortunate messenger turned a deep red; he clutched his helmet so hard Annabel was afraid it would crack and splinter.

"Got a delivery, have you?" Mark stared boldly at the parcel the messenger was carrying. "Give it here. I'll see the old sod gets it."

"Yeah, right." The messenger held on to the package. "Thing is, I've got orders to deliver it hand-to-hand."

"You don't trust me?" Mark challenged him.

'Course I do. But I've got orders." They faced each other implacably. It was an argument Mark was bound to lose; he was unable to stand up and physically wrest the package away from the other man.

"Fourth floor." He contented himself with a shrug and another sneer. "He's in the boudoir with his bint—and he won't thank you for bursting in on him."

The messenger gave a nod that said maybe that was true—and maybe it wasn't—and turned away to the lift.

"Anything else you want?" Mark turned his attention back to Annabel, the fury smouldering at the back of his eyes told her that she would not be forgiven easily for having witnessed his defeat.

"Thanks for the keys," she said. "I'll see you tomorrow."

"Mind how you go—" His mocking voice followed her as she hurried towards the door. "I didn't—and look what happened to me!"

5

When she reached home, Annabel mixed herself a shaker of martinis, poured a generous one and told herself Dinah wouldn't mind at all if she had a quick rummage through the boxroom to see if she could find anything remotely useful to convey her growing accumulation of decorator's samples to and from the Arbuthnot premises.

At first glance, it didn't look too promising. There were a few old trunks which were far too large and cumbersome, even the child-size one. That child! It just went to prove how dangerous parenthood was—one never knew how the child would grow up. She shook her head and took another quick swallow before looking further.

A couple of battered leather briefcases, obviously the property of the late Lord Cosgreave, were too small. Suitcases were unsuitable, as were the plastic carrier bags piled in one corner, although Annabel seemed to recall reading that those in the legal profession, in a burst of reverse snobbery, had taken to using plastic carrier bags instead of briefcases to carry their papers to court. Wouldn't do for her, though.

Then she saw it. In the farthest corner. Good-sized, woven of thin slats of wood, sort of a cross between a trug and a small picnic basket, with the added advantage of a lid hinged in the middle, so that one could reach into one side or the other of it without disturbing everything it contained, it looked both chic and casual, the perfect compromise between looking too professional and looking as though one had no professionalism at all.

Annabel lifted the basket and blew off the dust. A good wipe-down with a damp cloth and it would be ready for service. She carried it back to the kitchen.

There! It wasn't exactly gleaming, but it was not of a material that shone in any way. Thinking of which, she packed the paint charts and wallpaper samples in one side of it and the swatches of material in the other. Again, she noted the arrangement with approval, anything on either side of the basket could be concealed by just lifting the opposite side of the lid. That might be very useful . . .

Annabel crossed over to a cabinet where she had noticed a pewter flask, of the sort gentlemen carried to sports events so that they might ward off the chill, or restore themselves to a decent equanimity quickly and quietly if their wagered-on favourite should let them down.

She sniffed at it, rinsed it and then filled it from the martini pitcher. She screwed the lid and cup back on and then deposited it in the basket beneath the top swatches with a feeling of satisfaction. She was prepared for anything now.

She thought.

*   *   *

And she had been in such a good mood, too.

Even the non-appearance of Peter and Paul (they were starting their defections early) seemed unimportant. She accepted with a nod Kelda's explanation that they had another job to finish off first but would be back with Annabel as soon as possible.

Annabel had even been humming as she ruthlessly yanked down drapes which must have been *in situ* for generations, judging from the clouds of dust eddying out from them like a Saharan sandstorm as they hit the carpet—and that would have to go, too.

"You don't want those ratty old tassels!" Kelda swooped on the tarnished tasselled gold ropes, eyes gleaming. Beyond a doubt, she already had plans for them—and quality of that sort was almost unobtainable these days, certainly not at any price Kelda could afford.

"Oh, all right! Take them! No place for that old junk here!" Made reckless by a fresh infusion of decorating magazines last night (MINIMALISM RULES!; NO PLACE FOR CLUTTER!; A CLEAR VIEW TO THE FUTURE; DON'T BE DAUNTED BY TRADITION) and with only a faint disquiet engendered by the back-of-the-book trailers for next month's editions (THE BABY AND THE BATHWATER; IF GRANDMOTHER TREASURED IT, PERHAPS YOU SHOULD, TOO; NEVER GIVE UP ON THOSE OLD FAMILIAR BYGONES), Annabel told herself that Mr. Arbuthnot expected renewal, not restoration.

Of course, the best pieces would be kept. It had already been necessary to slap greedy hands away from several choice items but, on the whole, everything was progressing well.

Except for a strange uneasy feeling that would not go away. Annabel looked around, trying to pinpoint the source of her disquiet.

As had become usual, all doors except that of the room they were working in—and, of course, the Broomstick's—were closed. Occasionally, the Broomstick stalked down the corridor outside, sniffing disapproval, to answer the doorbell and usher yet another worried-looking stranger down to Mr. Arbuthnot's office.

It had been a while since the last visitor had left, wearing the usual dissatisfied expression. The whine of the lift signalled the imminent arrival of yet another . . . Why did she think of them as supplicants?

This time the doorbell did not ring. Instead, there was the scrape of a key in the lock and the soft click of the door closing. No footsteps, not even those muffled by the carpet. After a moment, Annabel saw why.

The wheelchair rolled past silently, its occupant grimly intent on his mission, a large parcel in his lap. The parcel was bright with EXPRESS . . . URGENT . . . flashes. Someone intended Mr. Arbuthnot to get it as soon as possible and Mark was going to oblige. He must consider it important, it was the first time Annabel had seen him move away from the reception desk. Usually, he piled any packages—even the ones marked EXPRESS or URGENT—on the edge of the desk and waited for the first person bound for the penthouse to take them up.

*   *   *

But that had been some while ago. Although Mark had remained with Mr. Arbuthnot longer than might have been expected for a mere delivery, he had returned to his post at least an hour ago. There had been no more visitors since, although Annabel thought she had heard Wystan's voice at one point and Tara's at another. Presumably they had used the inner staircase.

It had been silent for some time now. No one was around—That was it!

"Where's the supervisor?" Annabel demanded.

"What? Who?" Kelda looked bewildered.

"Sally," Annabel elucidated. "She was here all morning, but I haven't seen her for ages."

"Perhaps she got shut in one of the other rooms," Kelda said indifferently. "She's not here now."

"Obviously not." Annabel looked around again with increasing dissatisfaction. She had become accustomed to the friendly furry presence overseeing her efforts. There was a distinct feeling of something . . . someone . . . missing.

"Perhaps I'll just go and . . ." Annabel allowed the thought to trail off as she stepped out of the room and looked down the corridor, and looked at all the closed doors leading off it.

"Sally . . . ?" she called softly. "Sally . . . ?"

"*Now* what is it?" Not softly enough. The Broomstick erupted from her office, as though she had just been waiting for an excuse to complain.

"Shhhh!" Annabel held up her hand, realizing as she did so that she was fuelling the woman's fury. But she thought she had heard something . . . a faint answering yowl.

"Don't you shush *me*, you—you—" Incandescent with rage, Dora Stringer stepped forward to block her path.

"Sally . . . ?" Annabel sidestepped her neatly and continued down the passage, no longer bothering to keep her voice low. "Sally?" she called, pausing at each door and listening.

The plaintive yowl sounded closer. *Help,* it seemed to be saying. *Get me out of here.*

"Hang on, Sally," Annabel said. "I'm coming."

"Wretched animal! Always nosing about where it has no business to be. No! It can't be in there! That's Mr. Arbuthnot's office. The creature is never allowed in there."

Nevertheless, the yowling was coming from behind that door. More in deference to Mr. Arbuthnot's sensibilities than to the Broomstick's, Annabel tapped lightly on the door and waited for a moment before opening it.

"Mr. Arbuthnot can't be in there." The Broomstick changed her tune, no longer able to deny the noises on the other side of the door. "That miserable cat sneaked in—and heaven knows how much damage it's done to those sensitive machines." There was a note of subdued glee in her voice. "Now maybe he'll listen to me and get rid of it."

Annabel pushed the door open cautiously. She could hear Sally complaining bitterly somewhere in the office.

"Here, Sally . . . Come, Sally . . ." she called.

Sally answered vociferously, but remained where she was.

"She's got herself caught behind one of the machines! Mr. Arbuthnot will be furious!" Furious herself, Dora Stringer shoved Annabel to one side and barged through the door.

"Come out of there, you filthy little beast! Where are—?"

The scream was so piercing and sudden that Annabel recoiled. It seemed to ricochet from every surface, freezing her in her tracks, momentarily cutting off all coherent thought, almost deafening her. Annabel blinked and tried to pull herself together.

The scream went on and on, increasing in intensity. It was never going to stop. Sally's yowl rose in sympathy. The noise was unbearable.

One deals with hysteria by slapping the hysteric's face. Annabel fought with temptation and reluctantly won. She settled for pushing past Dora Stringer expecting, at the very least, to see total devastation, the precious computers a heap of smouldering wreckage. She was prepared to believe that Sally was relatively unhurt; no seriously injured animal could produce that amount of sound.

At first glance, everything seemed all right, the computers in place and undamaged, the work station in order.

"ARTHUR! ARTHUR!" The scream turned into a name. Dora Stringer hurled herself forward, falling on her knees beside a body lying on the carpet. "ARTHUR!"

How had Annabel ever got the impression that the apartment was deserted? Suddenly people were converging on the scene from all directions, in varying degrees of distress and shock.

"*ARTHUR!*" Tara appeared in the doorway to the study and rushed to kneel at his other side. "What's happened? Speak to me! Someone call an ambulance!"

Something about the way the eyes seemed to be glazing under the partially lowered lids made Annabel suspect that it was far too late for an ambulance. However, the formalities must be observed. She looked around for a telephone, but the only one available was connected to several other contraptions and she felt it would be safer not to disturb it.

Having crowded into the room, the others stood there frozen. Wystan stared down at his wealthy nephew's body in apparent amazement. Zenia moved closer to Neville, who abstractedly put an arm around her shoulders, although his speculative attention was centred on Tara.

"But—But—" Luther was shaking his head in denial. "He had his annual medical checkup only a couple of weeks ago. There was nothing wrong with his heart. The doctor said he was in tip-top condition. For his age."

"Wouldn't be the first time the quacks got it wrong," Wystan said. "I remember when old Buffy keeled over. Same thing—had got a clean bill of health only—"

"Wystan!" His wife glared at him. "Shut up!"

Everyone shut up except Sally. Her wail rose and fell, as though she were mourning the man who had been her best friend. She hovered over one out-

stretched hand, nuzzling it and howling afresh when
it did not move to pat her.

"Get away, you stupid beast!" Dora Stringer
snatched at Sally, caught her around the midriff and
hurled her across the room.

"You wouldn't dare do that if Arthur were still—"
Tara broke off her protest, looking horrified at herself.
She had nearly put the unthinkable into words and
made it real.

"*Do* something!" Zenia demanded. "Don't just
stand there! Doesn't anyone know the kiss of life?"

They looked at each other blankly. Luther's face
creased with distaste and he stepped back. Annabel
was riven with guilt and inadequacy: why hadn't she
taken that first aid course she had promised herself
last summer?

"I'll try." Kelda pushed forward and knelt by Arthur Arbuthnot's side, her body blocking their view
of what she was doing. Several hearty thumps suggested that she was attempting heart massage.

"For God's sake, get a doctor!" Zenia snapped.
"Call an ambulance!"

"Yes, yes, of course." Wystan started forward, then
halted, staring uneasily at the complicated telephone.
He extended his hand, then drew it back, looking
down anxiously at Arthur Arbuthnot, as though the
fallen tycoon might suddenly rise up and smite him
for his temerity. "Er . . . *any* ambulance?"

"Quite right—for once—Wystan." Zenia was re-
covering from her initial shock. She stared at her su-
pine nephew with a cold, calculating gaze. "Ring
Hopewell International Medications. They can be de-

pended upon to do their utmost for ... a majority shareholder."

For the owner of their company. Annabel made the translation effortlessly. The Hopewell chain of private hospitals and even more private nursing homes was well known to anyone on the fringes of the gossip trade. Their discretion—some might say secrecy— was legendary. Whenever an aged relative, neurotic spouse, stressed-out (whether from drink or drugs) celebrity needed to disappear for a time, one could be fairly certain that the doors of one of the HIM establishments had closed behind them and would not be opened until they were back on their feet and presentable to the public once again.

"Erm, yes." Wystan still looked unhappy. "Erm, what's their telephone number?"

"Never mind, I'll call them myself. From downstairs." Zenia started from the room. "I'll want to have a word with them, in any case." Wystan trailed after her, his face clearing now that someone else had taken the initiative. He did not look back.

Annabel desperately wanted to get to a telephone herself. It had just occurred to her that this was a first-class story for Xanthippe's Diary, possibly one that would wind up on the front page—and bring a tidy bonus.

"Go away!" Sally had begun creeping forward again, trying to reach her beloved master. "Away!" Dora Stringer stamped her foot and looked ready to kick out.

"I'll take her out of the way." Annabel gathered up

Sally, her excuse for getting out of there and to a telephone. "I'll shut her in the study."

Not being privy to her thoughts, no one moved to stop her.

"Come along," Annabel whispered to Sally. "You'll be safer with me."

"How bad?" Xanthippe was all agog. "Do you think he's dead?"

"Seriously ill, anyway. Perhaps in a coma," Annabel qualified. "See here, I can't talk now—they're all around me. I'll ring you from home tonight."

"Find out everything you can," Xanthippe directed. "Meanwhile, I'll send a team over to doorstep. Don't worry, they won't know who the tip-off came from."

"They'd better not!" Annabel replaced the receiver, then lingered, strangely unwilling to return to the crowded room where Arthur Arbuthnot lay. She glanced uneasily around the study, half afraid someone might have been lurking to overhear her telephone conversation.

But there was only Sally, prowling restlessly, obviously distressed and unhappy. What would become of her now, Annabel wondered. Apart from Mr. Arbuthnot, there did not seem to be many cat lovers around this place.

Sally halted beside the window and sniffed at the side panel that Arthur Arbuthnot had swept aside to reveal his hidden hoard of cash. The panel appeared to be ajar.

Annabel moved closer, staring avidly at the panel. Sally stretched out a tentative paw and dabbed at it.

What a good idea! Pawprints wouldn't show up the way fingerprints would and, even if they did, what could anyone do about it?

"Good girl, Sally," she encouraged. "Go ahead. See what's in there. It might be a mouse." She caught her breath as Sally attacked the protruding edge of the panel with determination—and success. The panel swung open, revealing the contents of the cupboard it concealed.

Rather, the lack of contents. The cupboard was bare—or as good as—compared to the way it had been crammed full the last time Annabel had glimpsed it.

The thick stacks of currency had vanished. The dollars, pounds, Deutschmarks and francs were gone. The safe had been cleared out. Only a few meagre bills of mongrel devalued currencies remained.

Had Arthur Arbuthnot emptied it himself, perhaps distributing the money to all those strange characters who had been visiting him lately? Or . . . Tara had entered his office through the door from this study. Had she improved the shining hour herself?

If so, did that mean that Tara had known Arthur Arbuthnot was dead, or otherwise incapacitated? Had she, perhaps, discovered the body first and decided to help herself to all that nice untraceable cash?

Sally sniffed at the nearly empty shelves, lost interest and backed away. Voices rose in the other room as more people came out of shock and began arguing about what should be done next. In other minute, someone might decide to come into the study and see what was going on here.

Annabel nudged the panel with her foot, trying to edge it back to its original position. To her consternation, it sprang forward and snapped shut with a sharp little click. She had used too much force. And now there was no way to prove that it had ever been opened and left ajar.

But why should she need proof? It was not her problem. Presumably, whoever was inheriting might be understandably miffed to think that a large portion of cash had disappeared from the estate, but it had nothing whatever to do with her.

"What are you doing there?" a voice from the doorway demanded sharply.

Annabel stooped and swept up the obliging Sally before straightening up and turning to face Neville and Tara. And that was another interesting question: where had Neville been in those moments before Dora Stringer began screaming? In here with Tara? They were both looking beyond her—to the concealed safe. Was it her imagination that they seemed to relax as they saw that the panel was firmly closed?

"I'm keeping the cat out of everyone's way," Annabel said coldly. "Just as I said I'd do."

"Sorry," Tara apologized half-heatedly. "I didn't mean to sound—We're so on edge. The shock. I still can't believe—"

In the distance a siren wailed. "Ambulance," Neville said tautly. "I hope it's ours."

From the office where Kelda worked over Arthur Arbuthnot, a muffled sobbing began. Somehow, it was unthinkable to connect it with Zenia. And Tara, Annabel noticed, was dryeyed. Was the Broomstick the only one to mourn Arthur? Or was she possibly just mourning the loss of what must have been quite a good job?

A soft plaintive cry from the furry bundle in her arms made Annabel revise her opinion. No, Dora Stringer was not the only mourner.

Nor the only one worried about her job, Annabel suddenly realized. If Arthur Arbuthnot died—assuming he was not already dead—what was going to happen about the redecoration? Her only contract was verbal—and with Arbuthnot himself. Would that be binding on the heirs? On the other hand, it was only too likely that the heirs would have so many other more immediate problems that it would take them some time to notice that she was still around. Annabel made a quick decision to adopt a low profile and continue with business as usual.

"They're here!" Tara looked around helplessly as the doorbell pealed sharply. The ambulance siren had cut off directly under the window just moments ago.

"Are they?" Neville seemed equally at a loss.

"I'll get it." Annabel started for the door, still cuddling Sally, who had begun trembling. She hoped the cat wasn't coming down with some illness.

"What's the matter? What are *they* doing here?" Mark blocked the doorway with his wheelchair, the paramedics immediately behind him.

"Mr. Arbuthnot has had some sort of attack. In the office." Annabel stepped back to let him roll past.

"Heart? Stroke?" Mark locked eyes with her momentarily before he moved. "How serious is it?"

"Very, I'm afraid." There was no point in denying

it; he would see for himself soon enough.

He cursed briefly and spun past her. The paramedics surged after him. Annabel followed more slowly, not anxious to return to the scene, even with reinforcements.

"Stand back!" Annabel heard a new, authoritative voice order as she approached. "Please, give us room to work. Give him room to breathe!"

To breathe? Was he still alive? Annabel reached the doorway just as Luther—the one most likely to respond to an order—began leading the reluctant exodus.

She stood aside to allow them to pass, then slipped into the office. Was Arthur really still alive? Perhaps that "give him air" routine was one the medics used to clear away onlookers so that they could get on with their jobs.

Certainly, it hadn't worked with everybody. Kelda was still hunched over the body, continuing her first aid.

"That's all right, miss." One of the medics gently lifted her away. "You've done fine. We'll take over now."

Seeming dazed, Kelda swayed on her feet. Was she going to faint? Annabel started towards her.

"So you got away!" Mark had wheeled his chair to Arthur Arbuthnot's side and was staring down at him, his face impassive but his fists clenched. "You got away before I could—"

"All right!" Kelda snapped back to life. She darted forward, grasped the back of his wheelchair and whirled it around. "They want us out of here—and they're right. If anything can be done, they're the ones to do it."

But was there anything to be done, except carry the body away? Annabel felt Sally tense in her arms as the wheelchair swept past them and Kelda met her eyes with a commanding glance.

Like Lot's wife, Annabel could not resist a backward look as she followed Kelda and the wheelchair from the room.

The paramedics had begun working in silent unison, not allowing themselves to consider the possibility of failure. More heart massage, oxygen mask, IV feed attached; they began doing other more complicated things Annabel could not even identify.

So intent were they on their task that they did not notice what was immediately apparent to Annabel as they gently moved the still form in the course of their ministrations.

There was a small dark-red stain on the carpet in approximately the centre of the spot where Arthur Arbuthnot's shoulder blades had rested.

6

Instinctively, Annabel closed the door on the scene behind her.

"Don't ever do that again!" Ahead of her, Mark twisted round in his chair and glared up at Kelda. He caught at the wheels, trying to halt their progress. But Kelda was stronger than she looked and continued to propel the chair ruthlessly along the hall.

Until she had to stop, her way blocked by the others in front of her who had gradually slowed their steps until they stood motionless in a huddled group, abruptly aware that they did not know where they wanted to go or what they wanted to do. Caught in a fresh wave of delayed shock, they might have been clockwork figures, losing momentum and faltering into suspended animation as their mainsprings wound down. Worse, their mainspring lay broken, perhaps beyond repair, with no power ever to activate them again.

The doorbell shrilled abruptly and proved that they could move, after all. They swung to face the door, then froze again, as though afraid of what might be on the other side.

"I'll get it." Dora Stringer moved forward, the familiar task seeming to give her a rush of confidence. She turned the knob and pulled the door open wide.

A flashbulb exploded in her face. She shrieked. Another flash, then another, the flashes forcing her back as the man behind the camera advanced into the hallway. Dora shrieked again and Tara added a yelp of her own, more the dismayed protest of a woman who realizes she has been caught not looking her best than a genuine sound of indignation.

"Stop that!" It was left to Zenia to explode with honest outrage. "Who are you? What are you doing here? Get out!"

The man swivelled and the flashbulb exploded in *her* face.

"Wystan! Throw them out!"

"Erm, Luther—" Wystan immediately looked for reinforcements.

Sally wrenched herself from Annabel's arms, leaped to the floor and skittered down the hallway, racing for sanctuary from all the flashing lights and the shouting.

"And hurry!" Zenia snapped. The urgency in her voice reminded them that the door at the far end of the corridor might open at any moment to disclose the paramedics carrying out their grim burden.

"Is it true—?" A young woman stepped out from behind the bulk of the photographer. "Is it true that Arthur Arbuthnot is dead?"

"Certainly not!" Zenia snarled.

"No comment," Wystan, the weakest link, said unwisely, not realizing that no comment was tantamount to confirmation.

"Mr. Arbuthnot has been taken ill," Tara intervened smoothly. "It's nothing serious. Overwork. His doctor is in attendance and he's resting comfortably."

Most probably resting in peace. Annabel moved back a few steps, hoping the journalists would not notice her. She didn't think they'd recognize her, but she had visited the newspaper office a few times and one never knew. They looked suspiciously like the pair she had seen rolling over the photocopier, hilariously recording improper bits of their anatomies at the Christmas party last year. Unreliable types at the best of times; one could not trust their discretion. She retreated more rapidly and found herself outside a door just beginning to open.

"Don't!" She slipped inside and confronted the startled medics. "Don't go out there! Not just yet."

"Oh, good." Neville had followed her. "You've stopped them. Good thinking." He gave her a nod of approval and she realized that she had inadvertently scored points with the family, although she had been more intent on escaping possible recognition than in sparing the family embarrassment. She gave Neville a weak smile.

"This way," he directed the medics. "There's a service lift. You won't have to carry him past the family and distress them." He did not mention the waiting paparazzi. "I'll go with you and make sure the way is clear. I mean, we haven't used the service entrance in some time. It may be locked, but I have the key."

He opened the door to the study. "Over there—"
He indicated a door on the far side of the room. "Tell
Mother"—he turned back to Annabel—"that I have
everything under control here."

The hubbub in the hallway seemed to have died
down. Annabel edged the door open and looked out
cautiously.

The photographer, the journalist, Luther and Wystan had all disappeared. Kelda had retreated along the
hallway and was hovering beside the drawing room
doorway, obviously ready to do her own disappearing
act.

Aunt Zenia and the Broomstick had now turned
their firepower on the unresisting Mark, who sat huddled in his wheelchair looking as though he might
explode at any moment.

". . . all your fault!" Aunt Zenia was seething. "If
you had been at your post, they never would have got
in here!"

"And those are just the ones who found their way
to the penthouse," the Broomstick weighed in. "How
many others do you suppose might have got in and
be sneaking through the building right this minute?
We'll have to search the place and throw them out!"
She sounded as though she relished the prospect.

"And what do you want?" She turned suddenly to
glare at Annabel, who had come up behind them.

"Your son said to tell you"—Annabel addressed
her answer to Zenia—"that he has everything under
control." She paused and elucidated as Zenia frowned
uncomprehendingly. "They've taken . . . him . . . down
in the service lift."

"The service—? Oh, my God!" Zenia sprang forward. "That fool, Wystan, told those paparazzi that he was going to throw them out through the tradesman's entrance because they're not fit to use the front door. They'll run right into each other! We've got to cut them off!"

"The backstairs! It's a slow lift and we might beat it." Tara turned and sprinted down the hall.

"Stay here in case they come back," Zenia directed Dora Stringer. "I'll go down the main staircase. And you—" She glared at Mark. "Take the lift and get back to your post!"

They all dispersed, leaving Annabel and Kelda staring at each other in the suddenly empty hallway. *Now what?* hung in the air between them.

"Ah, well," Kelda shrugged. "Back to business as usual." She led the way into the drawing room, marched purposefully to a corner where a loose edge of wallpaper threatened to peel away from the wall, slid her fingernail along the weakness, prised enough away to get a grip, took hold and pulled violently. A great flap of wallpaper tore away, leaving a wide gash across the wall.

"Don't just stand there!" she ordered as Annabel gasped. "Start stripping the wallpaper. They'll have to let us keep working then, even if it's just in this one room." She clawed away another large strip.

"No, I'll do this wall." She waved a hand, directing Annabel to the opposite wall. "Take that one—and work fast. We want this place to look terrible before they have a chance to stop us." She discarded the wallpaper on to the faded threadbare rug and kept tearing.

Annabel nodded and settled down to work on her own wall. Really, there was something almost therapeutic about this kind of destruction. One could begin to understand the pleasures of vandalism. After a while, the wall began to look better in its denuded state than it had when covered by that ghastly paper.

The pile of patterned strips in the centre of the rug grew to a satisfactory height before they paused for breath. No one would be mad enough to suggest that they go away and leave the room in its present state now.

With the silence no longer broken by the sound of tearing paper, it seemed to settle down around them oppressively.

"Quiet in here, isn't it?" Even Kelda seemed momentarily daunted.

"They've all got plenty to think about," Annabel said.

"Yes, but you'd have thought someone would have come by and said something to us—even if it was only, 'Get out!' "

Kelda was right. It was most unlike the Broomstick to miss such an opportunity for using her favourite phrase. There must be one hell of a conference going on somewhere. Downstairs, probably. Otherwise, there would certainly have been the sound of raised voices: this was not the sort of crisis any of them was likely to face with equanimity.

"They must be downstairs in Zenia's quarters," she told Kelda. "Unless," a new thought occurred to her, "some of them have gone to the hospital to be with—" But that was what a member of a normal family would do.

"Not them. Anyway, there's nothing they can do, is there?" Kelda was pragmatic. "At least they got him out of here. Now their tame medics can get it recorded that he died in the ambulance. Or, better still, the private hospital. Then they won't have the police sniffing around here."

"The police?" Annabel hoped she sounded more startled than she actually was. How much had Kelda seen? "Why should the police be involved?"

"Sudden death—without a doctor in attendance. The police will want to know what happened. Especially to a billionaire. That means an autopsy, coroner's inquest—" Kelda seemed to notice that she was being entirely too knowledgeable and broke off, shrugging her shoulders. "Who'd want to get caught up in all that? I don't blame them."

"And this way . . . a doctor will be present." Worse things had happened. Annabel remembered stories of dictators hitched up to medical machinery that kept their bodies technically alive for months and years. And there were other rich men who had died inconveniently and whose bodies had been transported by private jet to different countries in order to escape the complications of tax laws. As to what else might be covered up . . . she tried not to remember the dark stain on the carpet.

"They'll have a tame doctor who'll sign the death certificate without any argument. Then probably cremation. That would suit them just fine." How had

Kelda become so cynical in the comparatively few years she had lived? And had she also noticed the stain?

"Anyway," Kelda shrugged again. "It's nothing to do with us. We only work here."

"Quite right," Annabel agreed briskly. "And I think we've done enough for one day. Let's tidy up and go home."

Kelda nodded, shook open a black bin liner and began cramming in strips of wallpaper. Annabel watched her, still caught by a sense of uneasiness. Surely, someone should be coming to check on them after all this time, even if it was only the cat.

The cat! Where *was* Sally? Had she got shut into another of the rooms? And what was she shut in with this time? The thought would not go away.

"I'll be right back," Annabel said abruptly. Kelda nodded indifferently; she hadn't really expected help in tidying up.

It was twilight and the dark corridor seemed to stretch into infinity. Annabel found herself tiptoeing, curiously reluctant to make a sound. She paused by each closed door, whispering the cat's name, rather than calling it out into the silence. Cats had superior hearing; surely if Sally were behind the closed door, she would hear and respond as she had done before.

Before . . . Annabel shuddered and moved more quickly, anxious to find the cat and . . . And . . . ? Why was she so concerned about the cat? Was it, perhaps, that those moments when Sally had looked so trustingly at her had engendered some sort of feeling of responsibility? Or was it those other moments—

when cold eyes had stared down at Sally and feet had moved restlessly, as though to restrain a kick, now that her protector lay helpless—that had touched her own protective instincts? She told herself that she just wanted to make sure that Sally was all right before she left for the day.

She was at the end of the corridor, the door immediately ahead led into the study. (She'd think about that empty safe later.) The closed door on the right opened into the office. On the left, the door into the Broomstick's office was also firmly closed. Did the Broomstick have no further interest in what was happening outside now that her employer was no longer there to spy on?

Annabel hesitated, not sure which door to approach. Then a voice, low and urgent, "t . . . t . . . t . . . ," it seemed to be insisting. What on earth . . . ?

Without knocking, Annabel silently turned the doorknob and inched open the door to the Broomstick's stronghold.

Sally crouched in the middle of the room, alert and quivering, ready to spring upon some unseen prey.

"Get it!" the Broomstick was urging. "Get it! Go on, get it!"

Annabel stepped into the room. Now she could see the open window, the pigeon strutting along the windowsill, an insult and a challenge to any right-thinking cat with territory to defend.

"Go get it! Go on, get—"

"Sally!" Annabel shrieked as the cat gathered herself for the leap that would carry her out of the open window and—with or without the pigeon—down to the pavement six floors below.

"Wha—?" The Broomstick swung to face her. Sally, taking fright, bolted between her ankles and out the open door. "What are you doing here?"

"I—" Annabel kicked the door shut behind her so that Sally couldn't get back in. "I just came to say that we're leaving now. We'll resume work in the morning."

"Indeed?" Dora Stringer arched a contemptuous eyebrow. "Perhaps it would be as well if you waited for instructions as to when you might 'resume your work'." She turned her back on Annabel, one hand swinging out almost casually to slam down the window.

But not before Annabel had seen the bread fragments scattered along the outside sill. Her eyes narrowed. It was only a few days ago that this woman had nearly cracked the windowpane, screaming, "Vermin!" to drive away the hapless pigeons trying to perch on the sill. Now food was spread out invitingly, the window left open—and the cat was being urged to follow its natural instincts and pounce. With results that could only be fatal. No doubt about it, the Broomstick had deliberately tried to kill poor little Sally.

"I thought you said you were leaving." The Broomstick turned and advanced, ready to sweep Annabel out of the room, out of the flat, out of their lives. A cold glint in her eyes defied Annabel to challenge her, to voice what she suspected.

Annabel retreated slowly, her mind working quickly, already suspecting a lot more than she had a minute ago. The woman would never dare try to harm Sally unless she was sure retribution could not descend on her.

"How is Mr. Arbuthnot? Has there been any word from the hospital?"

"That's nothing to do with you!" Dora Stringer paused and seemed to regroup her thoughts. "Luther is working on a statement to be released to the media shortly. Meanwhile, Mr. Arbuthnot is doing as well as can be expected . . ."

. . . *of a dead man*. Annabel completed the sentence mentally. Arthur Arbuthnot was gone and his family and associates were fighting a rearguard action to conceal the fact until . . .

Until what? Until assets had been transferred? Until a Crown Prince had had time to seize the throne and make his position secure? Until a "deathbed marriage" had been arranged and staged? They were scheming something. But the Broomstick was right—it had nothing to do with her. All she wanted to do was complete the decorating, collect the agreed sum and get out of there.

". . . out!" The Broomstick completed some sentence Annabel had missed, but it was clear that they were two minds with but a single thought.

"Sorry I can't stay and chat any longer, but *some* of us have other work to do." Annabel spoke with deliberate intent to annoy and she succeeded. She closed the door against the satisfactory spectacle of rolling eyes and a mouth that looked as though it were about to foam. This time she allowed her footsteps to sound heavily and defiantly as she marched down the corridor.

She found Kelda trailing a long strip of wallpaper for Sally to chase. They both stopped and looked up as she entered.

"Are you all right?" Kelda looked mildly anxious.

"Fine." Annabel tried not to snap, no point in taking her annoyance out on Kelda. "Let's get out of here."

"Right." Kelda rolled up the strip of paper and rammed it into the bin liner under Sally's wistful gaze. "I'll load this stuff into the lift then."

"Don't bother. Leave it for the cleaners. Just take your own things."

"Right." Kelda gathered up the sack bulging with her gleanings. "Coming?"

"You go ahead." Annabel could not have said why she was reluctant. "I've got to get my things together. I'll see you in the morning. Meet me on the corner at ten. I think it will be better if we arrive together."

"One argument instead of two. Good thinking," Kelda approved. "See you then!" She was out of the door, with Sally still looking wistfully after her.

Sally. Annabel looked down at the cat and began to realize why she had wanted to stay behind. What was to be done about Sally?

"Sally . . ." A voice called softly along the corridor, as though echoing her thoughts. "Here, Sally . . . nice Sally . . . Come to Dora, Sally . . ." The voice was too sweet, insinuating, false. If Sally answered it . . .

Annabel wondered if Dora Stringer had opened the window again.

Sally looked towards the sound of the voice, then up at Annabel uncertainly. She moved over to brush against Annabel's ankles.

"Here, Sally . . . Where are you, you little beast? Sally . . . Come, Sally . . ."

Come and be killed. That did it!

"Shhhh!" Annabel bent and scooped up the soft furry body. It began to throb with purring.

"Shhhh!" Annabel warned again. She flipped open the lid of her basket, lifted out a wodge of fabric samples and lowered Sally into the basket. Sally blinked and began sniffing curiously at her new surroundings.

"Settle down." Annabel pressed gently on her back and Sally obligingly folded her legs under her and yawned.

"That's right—go to sleep," Annabel whispered, covering her with the fabrics. "We'll get you out of here and safe with me for tonight. Tomorrow, we'll see what we can do with you." The others were hostile or indifferent, but Tara had seemed to like the cat, even to the extent of bringing Sally a holiday souvenir. Or had she just been trying to curry favour with Arthur?

"Now just stay quiet . . ." Annabel lowered the lid, slipped the handles over her arm and left the flat at full speed. She noticed that she was tiptoeing again.

7

"You're in a good mood this morning," Kelda said, as they took off their jackets and began unloading rolls of wallpaper from the carrier bags Kelda had brought.

"Must be spring," Annabel agreed cheerfully, unable to confide the real reason. It was the relief because her initial fears about having a cat around the flat had proved groundless. Sally was the perfect house guest. After a preliminary exploration of her new surroundings, she had enthusiastically shared Annabel's cheese omelette. Later, she had accompanied Annabel to bed, where she curled up in a contented ball beside Annabel's shoulder and purred them both to sleep. This morning she had cheerfully breakfasted on slightly soggy cornflakes and settled down for a nap on the sofa. She was going to be no problem at all.

However, the fact remained that Sally belonged to Arthur Arbuthnot, or his family, and should be returned as soon as her safety could be ensured. Dora Stringer must not be allowed anywhere near her.

"Uh-oh." Kelda lifted her head and listened. "I knew this quiet was too good to last. Here comes trouble."

Annabel nodded recognition of the footsteps grimly thumping along the hallway and was prepared when they reached the doorway.

"Good morning, Miss Stringer," she said sweetly. "What news of poor Arthur today?"

"*Mr.* Arbuthnot," Dora Stringer frowned severely, "is still unwell." She stamped across the room, picked up one of the rolls of wallpaper and unrolled it enough to see the pattern. "No, no, no!" she cried. "This won't do at all!"

"I beg your pardon?" Kelda blinked at her.

"This pattern is quite unsuitable."

"But this is what Mr. Arbuthnot chose."

"Mr. Arbuthnot was under the influence of *that woman!* He quite forgot the original intention was to remodel this room into a business reception room. Flower-sprigged wallpaper will not do at all!"

She spoke as though Arthur Arbuthnot was coming back to continue his plans for his business and his flat.

"Just a plain beige paint, I think, with dark-brown trim and dark-brown drapes in a rough weave. Plain and businesslike."

"But Mr. Arbuthnot—" Kelda began to protest.

"Fortunately, I hold Mr. Arbuthnot's power of attorney and have done for many years. It was often necessary for me to make on-the-spot decisions when he was away on business trips." She took a deep breath and looked around the room with a proprietorial air, seeming to grow taller.

"So you see, all decisions are mine, now that Mr. Arbuthnot is . . . not in a condition to supervise arrangements himself."

She might be right. If Arthur Arbuthnot had had enough confidence in her to entrust her with his power of attorney, then she must be extremely knowledgeable about his business and who was to say that she might not have been left a sizeable share of it? Annabel reminded herself that she had walked in in the middle of the film, as it were. She had no idea of the prior loyalties or entanglements of these people. Dora Stringer clearly fell into the trusted-old-retainer category and it was obvious that she predated Luther, even though his job title was more impressive than hers. Those who held the titles were not always those who held the real power. It was probably better not to cross her . . . for the moment.

"If you want rough-weave drapes, perhaps you might like a textured wallpaper." Kelda had evidently come to the same conclusion; she smiled winningly at Dora Stringer. "Or use actual tweed material for the wall covering. It can be done quite easily, you know."

"Don't think you could charge any more for that!" Dora Stringer's eyes glittered menacingly. "I know Arthur paid you enough to hang the walls with ermine!"

"Well, hardly!" Annabel protested. "That was just a retainer. It by no means covers our fees and costs. Naturally, materials were not included; he hadn't even chosen them then." No need to let the woman think she could get away with claiming they had been paid in full in advance.

"Don't think you're going to get away with that story—" A telephone began ringing in the distance and Dora Stringer was distracted. "I'll deal with you later," she said, starting for the door.

Annabel and Kelda scarcely had time to exchange a silent raised-eyebrow communication before Wystan came into the drawing room; he must have been hovering outside.

"Oh, good." He looked around. "You haven't started yet. I came to warn you not to begin until Zenia's talked to you. She has some ideas of her own and you don't want to waste time on work you'll simply have to undo. She's tied up at the moment, but she'll be along as soon as she can." He gave them a nod and a wink and was gone.

"You know," Kelda stared after him. "People told me decorators had problems like this, but I didn't really believe them."

"In this place, I'd believe anything!" *Except that Arthur Arbuthnot was still alive*, Annabel added silently to herself. She wondered how much longer the others could keep up the pretence while the very way they were all jockeying for position gave the lie to it.

"Oh, there you are!" Tara appeared in the doorway. "I was hoping to find you here." She walked into the room with a solemn stately grace, a lace-trimmed handkerchief clutched in one hand. "I wanted to speak to you about the decorations."

"Really?" Annabel exchanged a wry glance with Kelda.

"Actually, I intended to sit in on Arthur's original consultation with you, but I've been so busy since my return from my holiday . . ." She let the thought trail off before continuing more firmly, "As Arthur's fiancée, I naturally expected to have a great deal of input on the choices made. After all, I'm the one who's going to be living here."

That could be true. It might depend on Arthur Arbuthnot's previous arrangements with the woman. (Somehow, Annabel did not feel that love had entered the equation—on either side.) A lot would depend on whether there had been a pre-nuptial agreement and/or whether Arthur Arbuthnot had made out a will in his fiancée's favour.

"Yes, that will do." Tara inspected the proposed wallpaper and was in no doubt. "After all, poor dear Arthur chose it himself to please me, didn't he?" She dabbed at dry eyes with the pristine handkerchief. Annabel wondered how soon she would exchange it for a black-bordered one.

"So you're satisfied with this wallpaper?" Annabel was anxious to get one firm decision on material already purchased.

"Well, I wouldn't say satisfied, but it will do . . . for now. I wouldn't want to go against Arthur's wishes . . ." Again the handkerchief came away from her eyes undampened. However, she managed a quaver in her voice.

"But—" Tara recovered briskly. "I do think he hadn't a clue about drapes—they're all wrong. I see the whole as more effective if the windows are sort of swathed . . . with sort of swagged bows . . . do you see what I mean?"

"Sort of," Annabel said limply. If these were the kind of instructions she was going to have to cope with, life was going to get increasingly difficult.

"Chocolate box!" Kelda snorted.

"Exactly!" Tara turned to her, pleased. "Something completely feminine and charming."

"A slightly formal boudoir." Annabel took a deep breath and tried to get into the spirit of it, wondering why the concept seemed vaguely familiar. Someone had mentioned the word before—and in connection with Tara.

"That's it! I was sure you'd understand. I'm not completely sure about the furnishings." Tara gave the chairs a well-deserved dismissive glance. "But we can talk about those later. I know Arthur has already paid for everything—"

"Not everything! Not by a long shot!" Where had everyone got the idea that Arthur had showered untold gold on his interior decorator? "Just a retainer and enough for initial expenses. The rest—"

"Tara! You're here." So was Neville and he did not appear pleased to see her.

"Neville." The smile Tara gave him was something less than radiant; she wasn't exactly delighted to encounter him, either. "I was just discussing plans for the flat with the designers."

"Yes, yes. It will all have to go, of course." He frowned at everything in sight. "Loft living—that's the thing these days! Open plan, height, light and space. We'll knock down the walls between most of these rooms, then break through the floor to the flat below, remove most of the floor—just keep enough around the sides to transform into a gallery area—perhaps take back the plaster to the brick foundation wall."

"But doesn't your mother live in the flat below?" Annabel could not quite believe what she was hearing. Did he plan to evict his own mother to facilitate his grandiose schemes?

"Oh, I'll take care of her," he replied ambiguously. "She won't have to worry about anything, you'll see. I've got lots of plans for this building."

"You might wait until it's yours!" For once, Tara allowed her claws to show.

"Bound to be," Neville said blithely. "Arthur had—has—too much sense to leave it to Mother; it would let us in for two lots of inheritance taxes eventually. Much better to skip a generation and let the business flow forward unimpeded. I've got plans for the business, too."

"I'm sure Arthur wouldn't think much of them," Tara said.

"Wouldn't he?" They exchanged a look they obviously thought inscrutable and he turned to Annabel. "What do you think?"

"I think I'm getting a headache," Annabel said faintly.

"Oh, you needn't worry," Neville said. "We'll get some proper builders in to take care of the structural alterations."

"Planning permission!" Kelda broke in triumphantly. "I'm sure you'll need planning permission for changes like that. It could take years."

"We'll see about that," Neville said smugly. "Meanwhile, I have no objection to your carrying on for the moment. Just don't spend too much money. It will all be temporary."

"I wouldn't be too sure of that." Tara's eyes narrowed. "Remember"—she said with peculiar emphasis—"Arthur has his own plans. You shouldn't forget that."

"There are lots of things we should remember." Now Neville's eyes narrowed. They regarded each other with cold speculation. "For instance, that little agreement we've had in place for some time." Neville moved closer and put an arm around Tara's waist. She froze.

"This is neither the time nor place to discuss anything." Tara moved away.

"Just the point I was making." He followed her to the door. "I suggest we adjourn to a quiet spot for a full and frank discussion." There was unexpected steel in his tone; Tara was not going to enjoy the discussion. They left without another word.

"What price being a fly on the wall for that little confrontation?" Kelda looked after them.

What price, indeed? Possibly a very good one from Xanthippe. Unfortunately, one had to be a bit clearer about the facts before reporting them. Again Annabel wondered just how true it was that Arthur Arbuthnot had intended to marry Tara; the woman could claim anything if she knew Arthur would never be able to deny it.

Annabel's first impression had been that Tara was Neville's girlfriend, yet he had cheerfully stepped into the background when Arthur was around. And what was the basis of the "little agreement" he had mentioned? Was it perhaps that Tara would marry Arthur and—in the fullness of time, it was to be hoped—become a rich widow, at which point she would then marry Neville and bring the estate back into the family? If she still wanted Neville by that time. Unless he had some hold over her . . .

"Has Wystan spoken to you?" Zenia appeared abruptly, looking around the room.

"Everyone has spoken to us," Kelda muttered. Not surprisingly, it went over Zenia's head.

"Very well," she said. "Then you know I don't think much of the wallpaper Arthur chose."

"Practically no one does." Kelda was in rebellious mood. Again, she was ignored.

"I want Regency stripes," Zenia said, in a tone that brooked no argument. "Pale gold. I'll want to see a wide selection of samples and swatches. Everything must be exactly right."

"But this is what Mr. Arbuthnot chose." Kelda, for some reason, seemed disposed to argue. "And Tara likes it, too."

"She would." Zenia sniffed. "Arthur was—is—always too easily satisfied." She turned to glare at Annabel. "I suppose you think I'm being unreasonable."

"Not at all," Annabel murmured. After Neville's ideas about refurbishing and updating, anything that didn't involve demolition and a flying trapeze paled into insignificance.

"Good." Zenia turned her hostile gaze to the bare walls. "I won't pretend I don't disapprove of this ill-advised plan of Arthur's but, since you've started, you might as well finish. Especially as I understand you've been paid in advance."

"That is not true!" Annabel felt her hackles rising. "Only the initial cost of consultation and some of the materials has been paid in advance. You will receive our invoice for the balance after the work has been completed."

"We'll see about that!" Zenia turned on her heel and stalked out, leaving an aura of impending lawsuits in her wake.

"I wish I hadn't given up smoking," Kelda brooded. "God, how I need a cigarette right now."

"Have a drink instead." Annabel rummaged around in her basket and pulled out her flask. "I knew this would come in useful. Here—" She poured into the flask top that doubled as a cup and handed it to Kelda. For herself, she took a swig directly from the flask. These were desperate times, need was urgent, and there was no time to waste trawling through the flat in search of a glass. Apart from which, she had no wish for further encounters with any of its inhabitants.

"That's better," Kelda sighed, holding out her cup for a refill. "I'm almost relaxed now. Arbuthnot is dead, isn't he? He must be, or they wouldn't be carrying on like this. Do they all imagine they're going to inherit?"

"Don't relax too much." Annabel caught the sound of another set of approaching footsteps.

"Good God!" Kelda heard them, too. "Who else is left?"

"Good morning." Luther slithered into the room. "Getting on well, are you?"

"That depends," Annabel said warily. "What do *you* want done here? Stripes? Flower sprigs? Zigzags . . . ?"

"Really, I couldn't care less." Luther looked carefully around the room—at baseboard level. "It's nothing whatever to do with me. I'm simply looking for dear little Sally. I haven't seen her all day. Has she been in here?"

8

Sally!

Instant guilt. Annabel hoped her flaming face might be blamed on the gin. She had forgotten all about the cat. So had everyone else. Luther was the first to come looking for Sally.

Strange, she had not pegged him as a cat lover.

"I haven't seen her today," Kelda said. "The last time I saw that cat, she was sniffing around the bin liners with all the stuff we were throwing out. That was last night."

"What?" Luther paled; he looked desperately towards Annabel.

"That's right," Annabel confirmed. "Sally was definitely nosing around those rubbish bags. Perhaps she thought there was something to eat in them." That much was true. Annabel snapped her mouth shut and forbore to add what she and Sally had done after that.

"Oh, no! This is terrible!" Luther stared around wildly. "You don't think—?" His voice rose to a squeak. "She couldn't have crawled into one of those bags and been thrown out with the rubbish?"

"Why don't you ask Miss Stringer?" Annabel suggested. "She might know something about it."

"Dora always hated Sally." Luther shuddered. "From the very first moment Arthur brought the poor little stray into his life, that miserable—Er . . ." He cleared his throat sharply. "Thank you. Perhaps I *will* go and see if she knows anything about . . ." His voice faded away as he slid out of the room and drifted down the corridor towards Dora Stringer's office.

"These damned flasks are always too small!" Annabel shook it impatiently. The thing was empty already.

"I move we adjourn to the nearest pub," Kelda voted sensibly. "We might even get something to eat there."

"Very good idea. Brilliant, in fact." Annabel replaced the flask under the pile of swatches and closed the lid of her basket. "Let us away."

"But it's not just Dora, you know." Unexpectedly, Luther's head popped round the door again. "They *all* hate poor dear little Sally. If you find her, you must bring her to me. Otherwise, I can't answer for her safety. Jealousy is a terrible thing!" His head disappeared again.

"Out!" Kelda grabbed Annabel's elbow and propelled her forward. "Quick! Before any more of them come back."

"What are you doing down here?" They were halfway across the downstairs lobby when Mark challenged them. "You're supposed to be working."

"Even the hired help gets a lunch hour," Kelda

said. "If you don't, perhaps you ought to join a union. If you do, why don't you join us?"

"Oh, very funny." Mark laughed; it was not a pleasant laugh. Kelda acted as though she did not hear it and continued to regard him gravely.

"Go to your lunch, then. Don't wait for me." He was suddenly savage. "I don't eat with traitors!"

"Who are you calling a traitor?" Kelda reacted immediately—to Annabel's relief. For a moment, she had been afraid that her own connection with Xanthippe might have been discovered.

"You tried to save the old bastard! Don't deny it—I saw you!" His mouth twisted in more of a sneer than a smile. "But you couldn't do it, could you? He's dead, at last."

"You can't know that!" Kelda fought against the very conclusion she had reached earlier herself. "It hasn't been admitted—I mean, announced—yet."

"It doesn't have to be. Look around you—everybody is walking on air, already planning how they're going to spend the money. They're so happy, I wouldn't be surprised if they hadn't finished him off themselves."

"You'd better not get caught making remarks like that," Kelda warned. "They could sue you."

"For what—my wheelchair?" He pushed viciously at the desk, propelling himself away from it.

"Mark!"

Annabel hadn't realized that one of the panels behind the desk was a swinging door. Mark crashed through it and was gone.

"There's a nice-looking little pub around the back."

Annabel carefully did not appear to notice that Kelda's eyes had filled with tears as she took her arm and led her out of the building. "It should be quick, cheap and cheerful."

"Why not?" Kelda blinked and raised her chin, but was still following her own train of thought. "Do you think it's possible that Mr. Arbuthnot could have been murdered? Or do you think that Mark is just trying to stir up trouble?"

"Why should he want to do that?"

"He hates them all; he blames them for his accident. Mark used to be a motorcycle courier—one of the fastest and best. So Arthur Arbuthnot used him a lot. About two years ago, he got a call to make an urgent delivery of documents. It was a cold rainy night, but Arthur Arbuthnot made a big song and dance about how important it was and promised him a bonus if he got there in less than half an hour. So Mark took chances, skidded on a turn and—" Kelda shrugged. "And now he's like that."

"Really?" Annabel tried to work out how many opportunities Mark and Kelda had had for exchanging confidences. It seemed to her that they had barely spoken to each other—until just now. "How do you know all this?"

"We've . . ." Kelda avoided her eyes. "We used to know each other . . . before . . . Oh! Here we are. How charming!"

"Relentlessly." The Bower had lush window boxes, over crowded colourful hanging baskets and rustic wooden seats outside mullioned windows. So had a lot of other pubs in London. Kelda wanted to change the subject. Annabel decided to let her get away with it . . . for the moment.

"Inside or outside?" Then she shivered as an unexpectedly chill wind swept around a corner. "Perhaps inside." Annabel answered her own question. "We can sit by the window and look out."

They collected gin and tonics and sandwiches and carried them to a window table before realizing their mistake.

"Perhaps this wasn't such a good idea," Annabel admitted.

"It isn't the greatest view in the world," Kelda agreed.

Across the narrow street, the rear of Arthur Arbuthnot's building was not so imposing as the front. The ground-floor level was almost obscured by the high wooden fence enclosing the areaway. It was obviously refuse collection day, for an array of black bin liners and garbage bins were piled along the foot of the fence.

"Not at all salubrious," Annabel mused. "At least we'll escape any smell from them." Now that she noticed, none of the outside tables were occupied, although the pub was doing a brisk business inside.

"Houses with Queen Anne fronts and Mary Ann backs, that's what they call them," Kelda said. "Not that there's much Queen Anne anywhere, it's plain ugly Victorian—How odd!"

Caught by her sudden change of tone, Annabel followed her gaze. Luther was closing the areaway door behind him and looking uncertainly at the heaps of rubbish awaiting collection. After a moment, he advanced cautiously and bent over. He appeared to be talking to himself—or, perhaps, to one of the bulging black bin liners.

"What on earth does he think he's doing?" Kelda wondered.

Apparently receiving no reply, or dissatisfied with the reply he got, Luther moved on to one of the garbage cans. He lifted the lid and peered inside, his nose crinkling but his lips still moving. Again, there seemed not to be the response he hoped for. He replaced the lid and nudged another bin liner with his foot.

"I'd say he was looking for something." Annabel was riveted. She watched raptly as Luther picked up one of the bin liners by its knot and shook it, testing its weight and possible contents.

"You told him—" Light dawned. "Kelda, you said the last time you saw Sally, she was nosing around the bin liners. He must think she got inside and was carried out with the trash. He's looking for her."

"But why?" Kelda shook her head as Luther lifted the lid of another garbage can, picked up a stick and prodded its murky depths. "He doesn't even like that cat. I've seen him stamp his foot to frighten her out of the room. In fact, I'd have said he hated her."

"That was my impression, too." Annabel frowned. There was the throb of a heavy motor advancing inexorably from the far end of the street. The sound seemed to drive Luther into a paroxysm close to hysteria. He hurled himself into the midst of the bin liners, nudging with his feet, picking up and shaking, his mouth working frantically.

"Sally . . . Sally . . ." They could hear his desperate cries inside the pub now.

The garbage truck rumbled closer. A couple of workmen ambled along in front of it. They were looking at him curiously.

Luther looked up and saw the men watching him. He dropped the sack he was holding and bolted through the door in the fence, slamming it behind him.

The men looked at each other and shrugged their shoulders, then began heaving sacks into the revolving maw at the rear of the truck.

"Well!" Kelda said. "What do you think of that?"

"I think I'll have another gin and tonic," Annabel said. "And not so much tonic with it, this time."

"Cold chicken all right with you?" Annabel asked needlessly. Sally had begun purring the instant the scent from the parcel Annabel was unwrapping reached her.

"Yes, I thought it might be." The warm furry pressure on her ankles was curiously heartening after the long day. It was very pleasant to come home to such an enthusiastic welcome.

Poor Arthur Arbuthnot. No wonder Sally had meant so much to him. His poisonous relatives almost certainly had never evinced such warmth towards him. Even now, their main concern was not his untimely demise, but the amount they stood to gain from it.

Had Mark any basis, except spite, for his suggestion that one of them had killed Arthur?

Not that it would surprise her. She had more than half suspected it herself when she saw those traces of blood on the carpet beneath Arthur's body. But then so much had happened so quickly and been so confused. And ever since, the door to the computer office had been locked, even though Luther spent most of his time working in there, so she had never been able to get back in and take a closer look at the condition of the carpet.

At her feet, Sally chirruped anxiously, reminding her that she was very hungry and that chicken smelled awfully good.

Sally! Sally had been in the office, a silent witness to whatever had happened. A witness who could never testify. But, possibly, one who could yet instil feelings of guilt and uneasiness on the murderer by the accusation in her eyes.

Was that why the Broomstick had tried to kill her? Why Luther was searching for her so frantically?

"Mmrrryaah?" The eyes were hopeful and trusting as they looked up at Annabel. *"Prryaah?"*

"All right, all right, I'm hurrying!" Annabel poured out a martini from the pitcher in the fridge and divided the cold chicken with Sally, but kept the potato salad for herself as Sally reacted to it with a disdainful sniff. She carried them into the living room and sank into an armchair but, before she had time to put her feet up on the matching footstool, the telephone rang.

"Annabel! I expected to hear from you long before this!" Xanthippe complained. "What have you been doing?"

"Eating." Annabel took another bite.

"For days? You haven't been dealing with other columnists, have you? Not trying to get an auction going, or anything? I would react very badly to that, Annabel. Very badly indeed."

"I never thought of such a thing." The obvious regret in Annabel's voice seemed to convince Xanthippe.

"Just as well. We have other sources, you know."

"Have you really?" Annabel's voice was frigid. She set her plate down on the floor by her feet and sat up straighter to deal with this barely concealed threat. "Then perhaps—"

"Oh, but you're the best," Xanthippe placated hastily, aware that she had gone too far. "You're the one on the inside. We're looking to you for all the gory details. Now that it's official."

"Official?"

"The flash just came over the Press Association line. It should be on the late-night newscast and all the papers will have it in the morning. Arthur Arbuthnot died this afternoon."

Died this afternoon. Did he, indeed?

"Annabel, are you still there?"

"What? Oh, yes. I was just thinking . . ." Annabel reached down for her plate to continue eating. Her hand encountered a small furry head. "Oh, you little rat!"

"Really, Annabel! There's no need to be rude!"

"No, no, not you. I was just talking—" Annabel suddenly realized that it might not be wise to admit to custody of a purloined puss. Not to a national columnist.

"I mean, I just . . ." She faltered. Sally had raised her head and was giving her an injured look. That plate had been placed on the floor, clearly an invitation to partake of its contents. How was she to know that Annabel had not finished with it?

"I'm sorry," Annabel said. "I just wasn't thinking." She was unused to sharing her home with a cat; she would have to be more careful in future.

"All right." Xanthippe forgave her graciously. "I've been called worse. But you can't fool me, you were thinking, you still are. Thinking what?"

"Isn't there a law that says a person isn't allowed to profit from a crime they've committed?"

"Crime? What crime? Murder?" Xanthippe pounced gleefully. "Annabel, you're on to something! You think Arthur Arbuthnot was murdered!"

"No, no," Annabel said quickly. "Nothing of the sort. It was just a passing thought." She didn't sound convincing, even to herself.

"A likely story!" Xanthippe jeered. "Come on, Annabel—give!"

"There's nothing to give. Nothing solid, nothing anyone could prove. Nothing . . ."

"Annabel, Annabel," Xanthippe wheedled. "If you've got suspicions, that's good enough for me. You know you've got a nose for scandal. Just keep nosing around, let me know what you find. Off the record, if you like, just as background material. We won't use any of it." Now Xanthippe was the one who sounded unconvincing.

"You're right there on the spot, Annabel. You'll see things. You'll hear things. There'll be a bonus,

Annabel, a good one, if we get a story out of this. Even if it's only suicide—"

"No." Annabel was sure of that. "It wasn't suicide."

"Then stay with it. Find out—"

At Annabel's feet, Sally finished the last shred of chicken and looked up at her speculatively.

"That's all there is right now," Annabel told her firmly.

"All right, then keep in touch," Xanthippe said. "And I mean close touch. Ring me tomorrow— whether you have anything to report or not." She rang off abruptly.

"So . . ." Annabel replaced the receiver slowly. "What do you think of that?"

Sally obviously thought that she could be more comfortable. She gathered herself and sprang into Annabel's lap where she curled up and began purring again.

When Annabel entered the lift in the morning, it was already occupied by a short man with a worried look, who was carrying an imposing briefcase. As she entered, he appeared to make a conscious effort to smooth out his expression; summoning even more effort, he managed a wintry smile. Above it, his eyes were cold and assessing.

Annabel curved her own lips briefly, no more anxious for polite conversation than he seemed to be. She had seen briefcases like that before; they portended no good.

He allowed his forefinger to hover over the top button and gave her an inquiring glance. She nodded. He pressed the button and the lift glided upwards.

The Broomstick was waiting when the lift doors parted. The man stepped back to allow Annabel to precede him.

"Oh, you needn't bother about *her*!" the Broomstick snapped. "She's just the decorator."

"Interior designer," Annabel corrected icily.

"Now, Dora," the man said. "Now, now."

"You're late!" Dora turned her firepower on him. "They're all here waiting for you." She eyed the briefcase greedily.

"I"—he checked his watch—"am precisely on time." He wasn't going to let Dora get away with anything, either. "Possibly the others are early."

"I'll show you to the study," Dora urged him on impatiently.

"I know the way." He was not to be hurried. He nodded to Annabel with more warmth than he had yet shown and set off down the hallway at a leisurely pace. Dora fussed along ahead of him, darting forward then coming back, like a sheepdog with a recalcitrant charge.

At the end of the hallway, he stopped and looked back. Seeing that Annabel was still in sight, he nodded to her again, but she had the impression that he wasn't really noticing her. He appeared to be looking for something else, or perhaps measuring the distance back to the lift.

He and Dora rounded the corner and disappeared. Annabel was still staring after them when she became aware that Kelda had been lurking in the shadowed door during the exchange.

Realizing she had been spotted, Kelda stepped forward and stared bitterly down the hallway. "What does that rotten little twister want now?"

"You know him?"

"He's the Arbuthnot hatchetman. Solicitor," she clarified, in answer to Annabel's puzzled look. "Lawyer, whatever you want to call him. Whenever there's dirty work to be done, Pennyman's the one who does it, waving his papers around to prove it's all legal, upright and above board. What he does may be legal—but it isn't right!"

"You do seem to know him." Annabel felt a mounting disquiet. It was becoming increasingly obvious that Kelda was no stranger to this establishment. They might not know her, but she certainly knew them.

"I should," Kelda said. "He was the bastard who came to Mark in hospital and told him he had no right to sue Arthur Arbuthnot because it wasn't Arbuthnot's fault that he, Mark, had taken reckless chances in doing his job. He told Mark that, if he tried to sue, Arbuthnot would defend—and he had more money to pay legal fees than Mark did. And then he said that Mark wouldn't be able to get legal aid to sue because—" Kelda's voice quivered between rage and tears.

"With Mark lying right there in the bed, he told him he wouldn't get legal aid because . . . because he hadn't a leg to stand on!"

"Oh, dear," Annabel murmured. "That was tactless. I suppose it was such a cliché that it just slipped out before he thought."

"He knew what he was saying!" Kelda was unforgiving. "Mark was helpless—and he was rubbing it in. Then he made Arbuthnot's counteroffer: Mark would always have a job with him and be looked after. It was the least he could do—but it made Mark feel like a charity case. He accepted the deal—he had to, but he's hated himself and Arbuthnot and everybody else in sight ever since."

Her eyes bright with unshed tears, Kelda whirled abruptly and marched back through the doorway to the drawing room.

Well! Discretion, Annabel decided, was called for. It was not a quality that had ever loomed large in her life, but Kelda obviously needed a bit of time to pull herself together. She had probably said far more than she had intended to, but the words had come spilling out once she had started. There was doubtless more to come and more questions to be answered but, for the moment, Kelda needed to be alone.

Besides . . . Annabel found herself drifting innocently down the hallway. Somehow, she was on tiptoe again. She pulled the tape measure out of her basket; such a useful thing, a tape measure—it provided both a badge of office and a measure of invisibility. An explanation for being anywhere at any time.

She turned the corner and was surprised, but cheered, to see a streak of light marking the study door. Someone hadn't closed it properly. The murmur of voices could be heard beyond it.

Annabel moved closer and studiously bent to measure the distance from the floor to the light fixture beside the door.

9

Just her luck, Annabel thought. All the way down the corridor and around the corner, she had been able to hear an unfamiliar male voice droning on in a monotone. Now that she was close enough to distinguish words, the voice had stopped and there was complete silence in the study. It seemed that she had missed whatever was going on. Or had she?

"I don't understand—"

"You can't be serious!"

"No! No! It's impossible!"

Suddenly, there was uproar. Shrieks, shouts and the occasional indignant phrase breaking through. Annabel began backing away slowly, poised to turn and run if the door opened any wider. She would hate to be caught eavesdropping.

"I suppose this is Arthur's idea of a joke!" Zenia's voice rang out loud and clear, absolving Annabel of any possible accusation of eavesdropping. She must have been audible three blocks away.

"How could you let him do this to us?" Tara was

turning on the lawyer, plaintive, but with a strident note in her voice.

"Mr. Arbuthnot had a perfect right to do whatever he wished with his estate. Such a bequest is not unknown." There was reproof in the lawyer's voice. Also, it seemed to be moving closer. Annabel retreated a bit farther.

"I'll want a copy of that will." Neville's voice was closer, too. It sounded as though he were following the lawyer to the door. "My own solicitor will want to take a close look at it."

"A not unreasonable request." There was a rustle of papers. "It's a bit complicated to take in all at once. I would, however, draw your attention to clauses nine through to thirteen. You will wish to study them carefully."

"Naturally, we intend to contest." That was Wystan, trying to sound in command of the situation.

"As you wish. It would be most inadvisable, however. Mr. Arbuthnot took that contingency into consideration. You will find that anyone who contests the will stands to lose any bequest already made to him . . . or her."

In the long and thoughtful silence that followed, the door opened and Mr. Pennyman paused in the doorway for his parting shot.

"Unfortunately—" His voice edged closer to elation than regret. "Most unfortunately, I have an important meeting in Edinburgh this afternoon, so I can't stay to discuss this further with you. I'll be back on Monday. You will have had time to digest all the implications by then. I haven't time now but, since I am the trustee, I will wish to meet the, um, 'heiress' and attempt to ascertain her preference for a guardian."

"But—" someone began to say, and broke off with a gasp, as though suddenly kicked.

"I'm sure we understand each other," Mr. Pennyman said smoothly. He turned and set off down the hallway at a brisk pace that threatened to break into a sprint at any sign of pursuit.

Annabel flattened herself against the wall, realizing, with reluctant admiration, the cleverness he had shown in coming to the family to read the will rather than having them assemble at his office. He had obviously expected trouble and it was easier for him to make his escape here than it would have been for him to try to clear a cluster of hysterical, squabbling legatees out of his office.

Mr. Pennyman cast an anxious backwards glance over his shoulder at discovering that the lift was not waiting and opted for the stairs, taking them at a breakneck pace. He was wise not to linger; already voices were rising again in the study and the rustle of turning pages sounded like dry winter leaves flying down the street before a gathering storm.

"Where is he?" Zenia appeared in the doorway, obviously the first to recover. "He can't leave us like this! I want to know—" Glancing over her shoulder, she stepped into the hallway and pulled the door shut behind her. A crafty look spread over her face.

"Sally . . ." she cooed. "Here, Sally . . . nice Sally . . . come to Auntie Zenia, Sally . . . Sally . . ." She moved forward and headed for the nearest doorway with a determined tread. "Sally . . . ?"

Behind her, she left chaos.

"I can't believe it!" Tara's voice soared above the others, perilously close to hysteria. "I just can't believe it! After all we were to each other—"

"Oh, yes?" Neville's tone was nasty. "And just how much 'all' was that?"

"I served that man for thirty years . . . I gave up any chance for a life of my own . . ," One had to feel sorry for the Broomstick, even though one did think that she had been a fool.

The diamond rings on Annabel's hand seemed to gleam sympathetically. Dora Stringer was now learning belatedly the lesson Annabel had learned a long time ago. The one about not putting your faith in the princes of this earth. No matter how truly princely they might be, they were mortal. They had a nasty habit of dying—and then where were you?

"I don't know what you're complaining about." Wystan's voice had never sounded so sharp. "He's left you a nice little nest egg. Not like poor Luther, who's got scarcely anything."

"Oh, I don't mind," Luther said unctuously. "I haven't been working for him very long, comparatively. I'm touched that he remembered me at all."

"Well, I mind!" Neville snarled. "Do you realize he's left me less than he left to that miserable broken-down motorcycle jockey downstairs? And I'm his own blood kin!"

"The old boy always felt a bit guilty about poor Mark," Wystan said. "One can understand it, but it's a pity he didn't consider his Aunt Zenia's feelings—"

"Arthur wasn't to know he'd predecease his aunt."

Tara was roused to a feeble defence; she didn't sound as though her heart were in it. "After all, she's older than he was."

"Yes, well . . ." Wystan seemed to take that as a personal criticism, as well as a reminder. She was older than he was, too. "Where *is* Zenia? She hasn't come back."

"That's right!" There was the sound of the door being wrenched open so hard it hit the wall. "Where is she? What's she doing?"

Suddenly, everyone burst into the hallway. Annabel was caught. Casually flourishing the tape measure, she bent and took a careful measurement of the distance between two imaginary points. Anyone could see quite clearly that she was far too absorbed in her work to have been paying one bit of attention to anything that might have been going on in the study. She hoped.

"Have you seen Zenia?" Tara demanded.

"Zenia?" Annabel blinked vaguely, wondering how much she dared deny. "I think she went past a few minutes ago. She seemed to be looking for the cat."

"I knew it! I knew she was up to something!" Tara started forward. "If anyone is to take care of dear little Sally, it should be me. Zenia doesn't even like her— and she'd have been *my* cat after I married Arthur. I'm sure that was what he was thinking about."

"Mmmm . . ." Wystan watched her hurry away purposefully. "Perhaps I ought to . . ." He seemed to fade into the distance.

Neville stood there dithering, obviously unable to decide whether to follow his mother or his girlfriend.

He turned to the others. "Has anyone seen the cat this morning?"

"I had more to worry about this morning than that bloody cat!" Dora Stringer said bitterly.

"Me?" Annabel was startled to find Neville waiting for a response from her. There flashed into her mind so vivid a picture of Sally settling down on her sofa with a contented purr just before she left the flat that she was almost afraid the others could see it, too.

"Sally wasn't around when I got here," Annabel said, arranging the truth as meticulously as a politician.

"No," Luther agreed. "Sally wasn't here this morning. I'm afraid I can't remember when I last saw her."

But he had been looking for her. Desperately. Only yesterday afternoon, Annabel had watched him rootling among the rubbish bins in the back alley, calling the cat. *Very* anxious to find the cat.

One did not have to be a mathematical genius to add up the way the family were behaving and to reach the conclusion that Arthur Arbuthnot had left most of his fortune to Sally, his cat. It had happened before, it would undoubtedly happen again. Eccentric millionaires did do things like that—not that Arthur Arbuthnot would have had to be particularly eccentric to prefer his cat to his poisonous relatives.

Luther must have known what was in the will; that was why he had been searching so frantically for Sally. What else did he know? He was looking suspiciously smug. Too smug. Annabel wondered just how much he was going to inherit. Even if it wasn't enough to retire on, he was still in a very good position. Young enough to continue making his way in the world, and a stint as Arthur Arbuthnot's personal assistant on his CV would be made doubly impressive by the fact that he had neither resigned nor been fired, but had lost his position solely because of his employer's demise. Yes, Luther was the best placed of any of them for onward-and-upward progress.

Unless, of course, he had been the one who killed Arthur Arbuthnot. That would be certain to discourage any future employer.

"Sally . . . Sally . . ."

"Here, kitty, kitty, kitty . . ."

"Come on, Sally . . . Good girl, Sally . . ."

The plaintive calls resounded from various quarters of the apartment as the hunt intensified. The original urgency was giving way to panic.

"Where is the hell-forsaken beast?" Neville demanded. "Where can it have got to?"

"If you ask me—" Even now, the Broomstick could not keep the grim satisfaction out of her voice. "The wretched creature has gone back to whatever alley it came from."

"Who asked you?" Neville snapped, quite forgetting that he had.

"Well, now," Luther murmured complacently. "If she's run away and lost herself, that would be most unfortunate. Most unfortunate indeed, as things stand."

"What do you mean?" Neville regarded him with justifiable suspicion. Luther appeared to be enjoying himself far too much, in his own quiet way.

"It looks as though Sally has disappeared." Luther's glasses flashed a spark of light as he turned to Neville with an unpleasant smile. "Wouldn't it be ironic if you had to wait seven years before she could be officially declared dead and the estate redistributed?"

By late afternoon, the hunt had spread to the lowest reaches of the building. The searchers had spent an inordinate amount of time in the lower part of the flat, unable or unwilling to believe that Sally would not have gone to ground in the bedrooms or kitchen.

"Here, Sally . . . dear Sally . . ."

"Come to Auntie, darling . . ."

"Get out here,.you filthy little bastard!"

Annabel's initial feeling of guilt had disappeared when she overheard a number of stray remarks which left no doubt as to Sally's fate when and if she were found. At best, the poor innocent would be torn apart as everyone squabbled over her custody. At worst . . .

"A dead cat can't inherit." Neville and his mother had paused for a quick consultation while they waited for the lift. "We're the closest of blood kin. No cat— and everything would revert to us."

No, the only recourse was to hold on to Sally until she could deliver her safely to Mr. Pennyman on Monday and let him take over from there.

"These people are crazy!" Kelda exploded, reappearing in the drawing room after a break for lunch. "Do you know what they've just done to Mark? Made him get up out of his wheelchair—all the way out. So that they could check it over. As though he might have been sitting on the cat—like it was a cushion and he hadn't noticed it was there."

"Incredible," Annabel murmured soothingly.

"I hope they never find it! I hope they have to wait forever for the estate to be settled! It would serve them right!"

"And what about Mark?" Annabel watched as Kelda stormed around the room, picking up brushes and putting them down, moving pots of paint, frowning and miserable. "Will he want to wait that long?"

"Mark has waited long enough already! Do you know—?" Kelda slammed down a roll of wallpaper. "The old bastard left him the exact amount he was going to sue for! That just goes to show, doesn't it?"

"Show what?" Annabel deftly removed a pair of scissors before the twitching hands could close on them.

"He felt guilty. Mark was right—it was all Arbuthnot's fault and he knew it, even though he kept denying it. If he'd only given Mark the money in the first place, everything would have been so different. We could have—"

Outside, the lift doors clattered and a triumphal shout blasted down the hallway.

"GOT HER! FOUND THE LITTLE BLIGHTER! HERE'S OUR SALLY, SAFELY HOME!"

Annabel was through the doorway and into the hall before Kelda had time to raise her eyebrows.

Uncle Wystan was almost jogging down the corridor, still crowing his triumph. Bouncing in his arms was a large placid tabby, who bore no resemblance to the dainty Sally, except for the mottled tiger fur.

"Oh, well done!"

"Splendid . . ."

"Where did you find her?"

The others converged from every direction, exuding relief and exultation. They crowded round Wystan and his captive, reaching out to touch the cat. Then they gradually fell silent.

"Um, are you absolutely sure, old man?" Neville was the first to voice disquiet. "She looks a bit, um, tatty."

"Isn't it bigger than Sally?" Tara frowned critically. "And there's something wrong with its mouth."

She was right, Annabel saw. One long sharp incisor protruded at an angle, twisting the cat's lip and giving it the appearance of leering.

"Coat's a bit rough at the moment, that's all," Wystan assured them. "After a night out on the tiles, you might not look your best, either. Er, that is, I mean—" He broke off, suddenly aware of extreme tactlessness.

"I don't think that's Sally," the Broomstick said slowly. "There's something different about her."

"But close . . ." Luther studied the cat admiringly. "Very, very close. If Sally doesn't come back, it just might work."

"Of course this is Sally," Wystan insisted, tousling the cat's already tousled fur. "Just look at the way she responds." A loud purring had started. "She knows us, all right. She knows she's home." He bent and deposited the cat lightly on the floor. "Just watch— she'll go straight to her food bowl."

The cat lifted its head and sniffed the air, then seemed to come to a decision. It sauntered away from them. It was heading in the right direction, but . . .

"Wystan, you fool!" Zenia screamed. "That's not Sally! That's a-a-a Salvatore!"

The cat swivelled its head and regarded them genially, as though acknowledging its name. When it swung away again, they all saw what Zenia meant.

"It's a male," Neville said. "No doubt about it."

Tara giggled abruptly, shrilly, teetering on the verge of hysteria. The Broomstick snorted in disgust and turned away.

"Ooh, ah." Wystan looked after the cat in dismay. "I hadn't noticed. The fur—The markings are so nearly right."

"Very close indeed," Luther affirmed. "Without the real Sally, you still might just get away with it."

"Nonsense!" Zenia snarled. "If there's one thing certain, it's that that bloody cat was a female." A calculating look crept into her eyes. "Of course, we might just . . ."

"Hmmm, I see what you mean." Neville was clearly a chip off the old block. "I didn't exactly get the impression that old Pennyman was a keen animal lover. I'd be surprised if he pays any attention to them at all. After all, they don't show up in court often, either as plaintiffs or defendants. He probably can tell a cat from a dog but, other than that, I doubt that he'd know one cat from another."

"Even so," Tara said. "Someone else might."

Salvatore seemed to sense something unpleasant in the atmosphere. He sat down abruptly, turning to face them, his tail tucked tightly around his body.

"We have until Monday," Zenia calculated rapidly.

"And there are plenty of veterinarians around. Just a few minor adjustments and . . ."

Salvatore began to look worried. He stared from one human to the other, but seemed to shrink as they stared back impassively. A stray cat was accustomed to the indifference of the world around him, wary of the random malice of bullies who would harm him, but ever hopeful that somewhere, sometime, some friendly stranger might rescue and adopt him and bring him in from the cold.

"It would have to be a vet from well outside the city," Neville said judiciously. "A country vet with a large practice, too busy to ask questions and with no time to read the newspapers or watch television . . ."

"Exactly," Zenia agreed. "It should be quite simple. A snip here and there . . . and that tooth would have to go . . ."

Salvatore looked beyond them and met Annabel's eyes.

Annabel shuddered involuntarily. It was as though she had just intercepted a cry for help.

"Bit hard on the poor old boy." Wystan demurred momentarily, then succumbed as his wife's stony gaze fell on him. "Still, all for the best, I daresay. Win some, lose some—he'll have a good home now."

"A short life, but a merry one," Luther murmured.

"Not all that merry," Neville laughed nastily, "after he's seen the vet."

Again, Annabel was conscious of an imploring look from the cat. She hoped the others hadn't noticed it.

They hadn't. They were all staring down at the cat, but without seeing it as a being in its own right. To them, it was nothing but a necessary pawn in their game.

Salvatore shifted uneasily and lowered himself to a crouch. His eyes scanned the territory beyond the forest of legs surrounding him. He had obviously been having second thoughts about his new friend, Wystan, and was about to make a dash for freedom.

"I don't know about this," Wystan frowned. Salvatore looked at him hopefully. "Even if we get the poor old boy done right away, won't it still show by Monday? I mean, won't the scars be, er, raw? Noticeable?"

"Don't be absurd, Wystan," Zenia said crisply. "You can't imagine Mr. Pennyman is going to inspect the cat closely enough to notice anything like that. The beast is the right size, shape and colour; we'll tie a pink bow around its neck and no one will be able to tell the difference. Certainly not a solicitor who has no interest in cats to begin with."

"You may be right," her husband admitted.

"Of course I'm right! Now, about that vet..." Zenia turned away, frowning thoughtfully.

"My cousin in Bedfordshire has a jolly good vet," Tara said. "She's always going on about how wonderful he is. Of course, he specializes in horses, but that's all to the good, he wouldn't pay much attention to a cat, either. I could ring her and she'd make an appointment for us. We could pop the cat into a box and drive down this afternoon."

Salvatore abandoned hope. He launched himself forward, dived through a gap between Neville's ankles, and scurried down the hallway, his paws barely touching the floor.

10

"Stop him!" . . .

"Get him!" . . .

"Head him off!" . . .

"Close the doors!" . . .

"Don't let him get away!' . . .

The confusion of shouted orders led to everyone moving at the same time, colliding with each other as they rushed to follow the cat, block exits, and recapture their victim.

Annabel backed quietly into the drawing room, bumping into Kelda, who was close behind her.

"Do you think we should try to help?" Kelda asked.

"Help *them*?" Annabel shot Kelda a look of such distaste that Kelda immediately backtracked.

"Or, at least, show willing," she qualified. "We don't actually have to do anything, just seem to be on their side."

"And are we?" Annabel asked icily. She knew whose side she was on—and it was not the side of people who were prepared to mutilate an innocent cat

while overlooking the possible murder of their bene-
factor.

"Well," Kelda said uneasily. "Luther could be
right. It might tie up the probate of the will for ages
if they can't produce the, um, main beneficiary."

Which meant that Mark would have to wait a long
time for the money to start his new life. And so, possibly, would Kelda.

"Go ahead, if you want to," Annabel said. "I have
quite enough to do right here. Speaking of which"—
Every good general knows the best defence is an attack—"where are those assistants of yours? Peter and
Paul—I thought you had them lined up to do the don-
key work for us. What's happened to them?"

"Oh . . . er . . . yes . . ." Kelda had started for the
door, but paused and turned back uneasily. "Umm, I
didn't have a chance to tell you, but we'll have new
helpers tomorrow. The boys had a sudden rush job at
the theatre, so they're sending along a couple of
friends to take their places." She sent Annabel a look
as pleading as Salvatore's. "Please, just don't say anything. Anything at all."

"All right, all right," Annabel said impatiently. As
Peter and Paul had not appeared since they had
cleared the hall of antlers, their presence did not figure
greatly in her life. "Just as long as there's somebody
to do the heavy work."

"Guard the stairs!" Outside, the sporadic shouting
erupted. "If it gets outdoors, we'll never find it again!"
There was a bellow and a thud.

"Stop playing the fool, Wystan!" Zenia was in no

mood to suffer fools gladly. "Get up and get on with it!"

"I tripped," Wystan whined. "I might have dislocated something. I've got to rest a minute."

There was an explosive sound of disgust, heralding Zenia's arrival in the drawing room. She looked around slowly, frowning at Kelda and Annabel. She seemed disgusted with them, too.

"Is there anything we can do?" Kelda asked nervously.

For a moment, it didn't appear that Zenia was going to answer; her gaze travelled slowly around the room at floor level. When she raised her head, her eyes were colder than usual.

"Find that cat!" she ordered. "And bring it to me. To me, do you understand? Don't let any of the others get it!" Her eyes bored into them, as though trying to hypnotize them to her will, then she turned on her heel and stalked from the room.

"Brrr!" Kelda shivered. "I feel sorry for that poor cat if it falls into her hands."

"As well you might," Annabel said darkly.

"Perhaps we shouldn't help them." Kelda hovered, irresolute. "But Mark . . ." She thought a moment. "Maybe I can look as though I'm trying to help—but I don't actually have to *do* anything." That settled to her satisfaction, she took off after Zenia.

Annabel sighed and slumped against the wall.

"Phwerrr . . ." A tiny little voice seemed to echo her relief.

"What?" She looked around cautiously, but not at

floor level. The sound had come from much nearer to her ears.

"Where are you?" she whispered.

There was no answer. That one small mewl had been as instinctive and involuntary as Annabel's own sigh. But Salvatore was back on guard now and lying low. But where? The room was stripped and bare, except for the pile of wallpaper rolls in one corner, waiting either a change of decision (for the moment, pale-yellow Regency stripe had won) or the arrival of the new helpers to hang it—whichever came first. No hiding place there.

Annabel held her breath, listening to the silence in the room. She could faintly hear the rush of traffic in the road below, the wail of a siren in the distance, the hum of the wind rounding the corner of the building. Then she heard it: a faint susurration of fur brushing against a rigid surface, as though someone was changing position slightly.

"Gotcha!" She crossed to the window in two strides and looked behind the half-folded shutters.

Scrunched unhappily between the windowpane and shutter, Salvatore looked up at her, half defiant, half pleading.

"You're all right," she said. "It's only me." *And I'm going to get you out of here*. She closed her lips over the sentence, afraid someone might hear her talking in an empty room and come to investigate.

Her thought seemed to convey itself to Salvatore. He stretched his neck forward and gently nuzzled her hand. The little snaggle tooth brushed against her fingers, the sensation was not unpleasant. The tooth obviously didn't bother him, he had learned to live with it comfortably. He was a perfectly healthy, happy cat. At least, he would be happy again once he got out of here. It was unthinkable that those ghastly people should be allowed to mutilate him to serve their own purposes.

"Come along." She slid her hand under his body and tried to lift him free of the shutters. He didn't help, but he didn't try to hinder, either. He went limp, as though he had resigned himself to whatever fate had in store.

Annabel felt the weight of almost too much responsibility. But what else could she do? Salvatore trusted her and she could not let him down. Nor could she return him to the streets, where they might find him again. After all, what was the worst any of them could do to her if they caught her making off with the cat? Fire her, that was all. And it would be no hardship to be rid of this place.

"*Shhh-shhh . . .*" she crooned, opening the lid of her basket and lowering Salvatore into it, draping a swathe of dotted muslin over him. He wriggled uncomfortably and she burrowed beneath him to rescue her flask. And that wasn't such a bad idea.

She unscrewed the cap and raised the flask to her lips for one quick swig before continuing their escape.

"I say, have you seen—? Oops! Sorry!" Neville stood awkwardly in the doorway, staring with fascination at the flask.

"Yes?" Annabel eyed him coldly, lowering the flask. No point in pretending it wasn't there. She screwed on the cap, rather wishing she had been ladylike enough to have poured her martini into that first, and replaced it in the basket, which gave her the opportunity to check that Salvatore was completely concealed by the material. He was. She shut the lid and faced Neville haughtily. "What was it you wanted?"

"Oh, er . . ." From the wistful expression on his face, a chance at the flask for himself would not have come amiss. "I was looking for Tara. I, um, don't suppose you've seen her?"

"I have not seen anyone—although I have certainly *heard* everyone!" Annabel drew herself up and passed the back of one hand across her forehead in what she hoped was a suitably distraught manner. "The noise levels around this place have been appalling and quite unacceptable! How is one expected to be able to create in such a madhouse?"

She stooped and picked up her basket, balancing it carefully and hoping Salvatore would not do anything to give them away.

"I can't work in such chaos! In the unlikely event that anyone should be looking for me, I shall be at home, composing myself for the morning when my new assistants will be here. And I trust the rest of you will have yourselves under control by then!"

As she had hoped, the artistic temperament card had been the right one to play.

"Of course, of course. I'm terribly sorry." Neville backed hastily out of her way, allowing her to sweep from the room.

Fortunately, the lift was waiting at the end of the corridor and she did not break stride or look back as she jabbed at the button and whisked inside the instant the doors opened wide enough.

She thanked her stars to find the entrance hall deserted; not even Mark sat at his post. Taking no chances, she charged through, looking neither left nor right, swung through the front door and across the pavement and hailed a taxi, sinking into the seat nearly as limp with relief as poor Salvatore.

Never had the front door of Lady Cosgreave's flat looked so welcoming. Annabel stepped inside gratefully and deposited her basket on the floor. Salvatore had been getting increasingly restless during the long taxi ride and now he ventured a soft, *"Meerroww?"*

Sally, who had come to greet her, promptly abandoned Annabel's ankles and turned to investigate the basket. *"Mmmmrrraa?"* she inquired, in her turn.

"Mrraaah!" The lid popped open suddenly, startling Sally. She skidded to a safe distance away and crouched, watching.

Annabel tensed. She had not given sufficient thought to whether or not the cats would get on together. She seemed to remember something she had read in the distant past to the effect that the best way to break up a cat fight was to throw a glass of water over the combatants. But a lot of fur could fly before she got to the kitchen and back again with the water. She wondered whether emptying the flask of martinis over them would have the same result.

She needn't have worried. Salvatore's head rose slowly above the rim of the basket and turned unhurriedly, surveying this new territory. Then he tilted his head ceilingwards, sniffing the air.

Annabel found herself inhaling deeply in sympathy. She had never noticed before how thoroughly Lady Cosgreave's expensive Parisian scent had permeated the atmosphere. Her own lighter, less expensive but deeply loved, floral scent floated on top of it. And heaven alone knew what secret feline messages were drifting out from the lovely Sally.

Salvatore lowered his head and looked around again. It was a dwelling place of females. Friendly females. His muscles seemed to relax and his facial expression became an affable leer.

Salvatore, you lucky devil, he seemed to be saying to himself, *you've landed in a tub of butter.*

He shook himself, smoothing his fur down, and leaped out of the basket. After twining appreciatively around Annabel's ankles, he sauntered over to Sally. They regarded each other solemnly for a moment, then stretched out and touched noses delicately. They seemed to commune silently, then Sally, flirting her whiskers, rose and stretched luxuriously and led the way into the kitchen.

Annabel trailed after them, feeling slightly superfluous. They were going to get along beautifully. Perhaps they had known each other back in the old days in the alley.

After one questioning glance at the complacent Sally, Salvatore hurled himself at the bowl of dried cat food with an eagerness that betrayed his hunger. Wystan must have captured him as he had been foraging for his next meal among the dustbins. Sally looked on benevolently, secure in the knowledge that a more appetizing meal would soon be on offer now that Annabel was home. She tilted her head at Annabel expectantly.

"Sautéed chicken livers on toast, I thought," Annabel responded. "The toast is for me, of course."

Salvatore lifted his head from the bowl momentarily and gave a loud purr of approval. Somewhere, there had been a word he recognized, or perhaps he had tuned in to the image in Annabel's mind of chopped onions and chicken livers sizzling in the frying pan—and the further image of most of them being divided into two saucers and set down on the floor.

Annabel removed the tub of chicken livers from the fridge and checked that they had thawed during her absence. They had been neatly cleaned and trimmed before being frozen, so they were all ready for cooking. What a pity that Lady Cosgreave's hospitality hadn't extended to retaining her excellent housekeeper for Annabel's term of residence. On the other hand, perhaps that was just as well. She would not like to have to explain just what she thought she was doing to a disapproving housekeeper, especially since she wasn't sure she knew that herself.

Salvatore had licked every last crumb from Sally's bowl. He looked at Annabel and, obviously realizing that it was going to be a little while before anything more was forthcoming, took a stroll around the kitchen and then headed out into the hallway. Sally padded after him.

"That's right, give him the guided tour," Annabel

grumbled. "It would be a shame if he missed anything."

Sally paused and looked over her shoulder at Annabel, seeming to smile in agreement.

Agreement! A cat! She was going out of her mind.
She *had* gone out of her mind. She was personally
responsible for removing a cat worth unknown mil-
lions of pounds from its lawful—very lawful; in fact,
it presumably owned the premises—abode. She had
also catnapped Salvatore, who was worth, perhaps,
fifty pence on a good day—although he didn't look
as though he'd had many of those lately, so perhaps
she needn't worry unduly about him.

There was no doubt about it, she was completely
and utterly out of her mind. She hoped that would be
a viable defence, when and if she were caught.

Annabel opened the fridge and poured herself a
martini from the waiting pitcher, then snatched up an
onion and began to chop it furiously.

11

Annabel awoke in the morning to discover two pairs of small eyes blinking at her fondly, two soft furry bodies pressed against her own, one on either side.

"Good morning, little chums," she said, then felt slightly foolish, but only for a moment.

Sally stretched out her neck to plant a delicate kiss on Annabel's cheek. Salvatore extended a protective possessive foreleg to lie across her ribcage. The sound of gentle purring intensified. Good morning? It was a splendid morning.

Annabel felt ridiculously happy; in another minute, she would begin purring herself. Wouldn't it be nice to spend the morning lying here contentedly, playing with the cats and not worrying about anything else in the world?

The world! Suddenly, it all rushed back to her. Her little chums had been illicitly acquired, her employer had most probably been murdered, her principal outlet for gossip tips was pushing for more information than she was willing, or able, to supply, and her financial situation—

Annabel sat up abruptly, tumbling the cats away from her and threw back the covers. The purrs changed to a duet of protest.

"Sorry about that," Annabel apologized, feet sliding into her slippers. "Who's for breakfast?"

The word was recognized and instant forgiveness ensued, with furry bodies twining around her ankles as she drew back the curtains and sunshine flooded into the bedroom. An omen for a good day, she hoped.

She led the parade into the kitchen, where generous dollops of last night's leftovers sent the cats into a state of bliss.

She smiled down at them. There was a pet shop nearby, she must make a small detour on her way to or from Regent's Park and pick up a little treat for them. Perhaps a catnip mouse . . .

The telephone interrupted her pleasant train of thought.

"What are you doing there?" The voice ringing down the line was loud, indignant, haranguing—unmistakably the Broomstick's. "You ought to be here! Controlling your workers! They're tearing the place apart. They've only been here ten minutes and they've already broken a window. You should be sued!"

"Workers—?" But the Broomstick had slammed down the telephone. Belatedly, Annabel remembered that Kelda had said something about new helpers starting work today. She stabbed out Kelda's telephone number, but there was no answer.

A deep foreboding settled over her. She returned to the kitchen only long enough to refill her flask with the martini mixture from the pitcher in the fridge. If the day continued the way it was going, they would be needed. So much for hopeful omens.

Kelda and the Broomstick were both waiting to intercept Annabel as she stepped out of the lift. Mark must have notified them of her arrival downstairs.

"I insist that you get rid of these people immediately!" Dora Stringer confronted her head-on. Behind Dora's back, Kelda was making frantic signals that Annabel could not interpret.

From farther down the hallway, a great pounding and banging was going on. Far too much noise when the main job to be done was to hang some wallpaper.

"I locked them in the antechamber," Dora Stringer pronounced righteously. "Before they could do any more damage."

There was something disquietingly familiar about the raised voices coming from behind the locked door. Annabel held out her hand, palm upwards, directly in front of Dora Stringer. After a long moment, the woman dropped the key into it.

"Keep them under control!" she demanded, retreating with hands on hips to watch from a safe distance.

"Stand back!" Annabel called. "I'm opening the door."

There was an abrupt silence, during which they could hear the scrape of the key turning, then the door was wrenched open from the other side, pulling Annabel off balance.

"Let me at her! I'm going to kill her!"

"No, you're not! I am!"

Annabel was jostled aside as two demented figures burst from their imprisonment and charged towards the Broomstick.

Annabel took a considered step backwards and thrust out her foot. The man went sprawling, catching the woman as he fell and taking her with him.

"Disgraceful! They're probably drunk, too!" The Broomstick surveyed the melee with grim relish. "They should be dismissed immediately!"

"I'll deal with them, thank you," Annabel said crisply. As she had suspected, they were the journalists who had forced their way into the building a few days ago. Xanthippe's minions. And now they were back, masquerading as part of the decorating team. Annabel gave her own minion a withering glare.

"I'll explain," Kelda said frantically. "Just don't—" She broke off. To finish the sentence would be to give the game away to the listening Broomstick.

"They're only temporary," Annabel assured Dora Stringer, baring her teeth at her, then turning the bared teeth warningly on Kelda and on the two suddenly subdued paparazzi, who had belatedly remembered their cover stories. "We just got them in to do the rough work."

Sudden disquiet flared in the watching eyes. "Now, wait a minute—" the woman began.

"They're going to take up the carpet," Annabel said firmly. "Then scrub the floor—and possibly sand it. Don't worry, they're going to be too busy to get into any more mischief."

"Er . . ." Kelda said nervously, as disquiet turned

to naked horror in the watching eyes and lips began to mouth silent threats.

"Either that, or they can leave now." Annabel was certain that they would rather do as she said than go back and face Xanthippe. In this case, the devil they didn't know was better than the devil they did. It was probably untrue that Xanthippe drank the blood of victims who had failed her, but it had been many a long day since anyone had cared to put it to the test. These two weren't going to.

"Very well." Dora Stringer capitulated suddenly, turning on her heel. "I have more to do than stand around here supervising the pathetic inadequates who work for you. On your head be it, if we have any more trouble from them."

They watched her stalk down the corridor and disappear into her office, then three pairs of eyes turned to regard Annabel warily. Annabel stared back implacably.

"Umm . . ." Kelda ventured. "I don't think you've met Cindy and Sid. They're . . ."

"I know who they are," Annabel said coldly. "And I know *what* they are"

"So what are you going to do about it?" Sid challenged her directly.

"I'm not—you are. You can start in the far corner, move carefully and try not to raise too much dust. The carpet—" she answered their uncomprehending looks. "Roll up the carpet—and watch out for the carpet tacks."

"You're joking!" Cindy gasped.

"Not at all. The Victorians were very keen on carpet tacks. Most of them must be quite rusty by now."

"Annabel—" Kelda tried to intervene. "I don't think—"

"So I've noticed!" Annabel's look sent Kelda backing away.

"Wait a minute." Cindy's eyes narrowed. "Don't I know you? I've seen you somewhere before."

"That's right," Sid agreed. "Didn't we doorstep her a couple of years ago? What was it . . . ? Yeah!" He snapped his fingers.

"The Black Widow! They got you after you offed your fourth husband. How come you're out so soon? I thought they put you away for a good twenty years."

"Very funny," Annabel said. "Now get started on that carpet. And after that you can scrub down the walls."

"Annabel!" Kelda wailed. "You're making a terrible mistake."

"She sure is." Sid rummaged in something that looked like a lunchbox and brought out a small camera. "You just sort her out while we get on with it."

"Given up the photocopier, have you?" Annabel stared pointedly at the camera. "What a pity. You were doing some very . . . innovative . . . work on it. I believe I still have a few copies. What did you do with the rest of them—send them out as Christmas cards?"

"What?" Sid let the camera slide back into the lunchbox. "Who are you?"

"Shall we say . . . a friend of the management? Your management. Have you shown them your interesting experiments? They could give new meaning to Page Three."

"I've changed my mind," Cindy announced abruptly. "I don't want to throttle that old bitch down the hall any more. This one is top of my list now."

"Business first," Annabel said briskly. "Playtime afterwards. Now, get at that carpet!"

She waited until they had reluctantly stooped to the task, then turned to Kelda. "And you—I'll speak to you in the study. Come along!"

They had barely reached the study when Wystan appeared.

"Oh, erm, I was just looking for Zenia," he said unconvincingly. It was probably Zenia who had sent him up to see what was going on.

"You won't find her here!" Annabel swung to face him, not bothering to adjust the laserbeam glare that had been piercing Kelda; he quailed as the full force of it struck him. Kelda took the opportunity to retreat a few steps.

"Oh, no? Erm, perhaps not." He twitched visibly, evidently torn between facing a furious Annabel or an implacable Zenia. "Just the same," he added more firmly, obviously coming down on the side of not further annoying the woman he had to live with. "I think I'll just look around a bit."

"As you like." Annabel turned back to block Kelda's escape route. That young woman had a great deal of explaining to do before she was allowed to get away.

"Ah! Right!" Realizing that her attention was diverted, Wystan slid away.

"As I was saying before we were interrupted—" Annabel advanced on the hapless Kelda. "How much? How much did they pay you?"

"Not a lot," Kelda quavered. "Hardly anything, really."

"How much?"

"They haven't actually paid me anything yet." Kelda tried to look pathetic. "It was only a promise."

"How much?"

"Five hundred pounds," Kelda admitted.

"Chicken feed," Annabel sneered.

"Per day," Kelda defended. "For every day they're allowed free access to the premises."

Annabel drew a deep breath. That was beyond anything Xanthippe had paid her . . . to date. Either Xanthippe was counting on this as a big international story, or Kelda had hidden depths as a negotiator. In fact, there was quite a lot about Kelda that might repay a closer look . . .

"I say—" Uncle Wystan reappeared in the doorway. "That female in there looks strangely familiar. Haven't I seen her before?"

"Not knowing the range of your female acquaintanceships," Annabel quelled him, "I couldn't say."

"Ah! Well!" He retreated backwards. "It was only a thought. Can't be sure. Can't be sure at all."

"I think they're from out of town," Kelda said impulsively. She caught Annabel's eyes. "But I can't be sure," she echoed.

"Always difficult," he sympathized with her. "So many of these females look alike nowadays. Practically in uniform. Hard to tell them apart.

"Not you, of course," he assured Kelda anxiously, as though afraid he might have offended her. Nor you," he assured Annabel. "Different generation entirely—"

Annabel raised an eyebrow.

"I mean—" He worked his mouth violently, like a man who had suddenly and inexplicably found his foot in it again. "Well, still looking for Zenia!" He turned and bolted away.

"I'll help you look!" Kelda dodged past Annabel and bolted after him.

Annabel let her go; she would deal with that young lady later. The first priority must be to keep the Arbuthnot heirs from realizing that the paparazzi were in their midst. They would then have the perfect excuse for cancelling the decorating contract. Instantly. And with extreme prejudice. The Broomstick would take care of that.

Annabel shuddered and determined to keep her unwilling helpers so busy that they had no time for prying and spying. She went back to the drawing room and looked in on them.

Sid was propped up against the wall, groaning. The carpet was in the middle of the room, half rolled up. Cindy was kicking ineffectually at the carpet, trying to roll it along.

"That's no good," Annabel said crisply. "You've got to put your back into it."

"You!" Sid turned to face her, wincing. "This is all your fault. I've gone and done me back in." He rubbed the small of his back, wincing some more.

"Sid hasn't lifted anything heavier than a camera

in years," Cindy said accusingly. "You're killing him."

"That would be too much to hope for!" Annabel regarded them both coldly. "If you're not up to the job, you can always leave."

"Not until we've got our money's worth." Cindy pouted belligerently. "That other one"—she obviously meant Kelda—"promised us we'd have a free hand."

"The promise wasn't hers to make. In any case, I can't see what you hope to gain by this. Nothing is happening here now. Arthur Arbuthnot is dead. It's all over. The parade's gone by."

"We have information otherwise," Cindy smirked.

"Yeah," Sid agreed. "We've got a friend at court in here somewhere. The tip-off is that there's a big story breaking."

With a guilty start, Annabel realized that they were talking about her. Xanthippe had sent them here to follow up on her own carelessly dropped hint about murder. Something she was powerless to prove and unable to investigate—and which might not even have happened. Had Xanthippe told Cindy and Sid what they should be looking for? At any rate, they did not appear to know the source of the tip-off—and Annabel intended to keep it that way.

"If you're planning to hang around here until something happens," Annabel said, "you're in for a long wait. Meanwhile, I suggest you finish rolling up that carpet and stand it up in the corner over there."

"Now, wait a minute—" Sid began.

"What's going on here?" Zenia stepped into the room. "Who are these people?"

"Temporary help. The others are down with flu. If these two don't work out, we won't have them back tomorrow." Annabel watched with grim satisfaction as Cindy and Sid stooped to the carpet and began pushing it energetically.

"They don't look very expert," Zenia said critically.

"They'll learn." Annabel tried for a diversion. "Have you seen your husband? He was in here looking for you a few minutes ago."

"Really?" Zenia shrugged indifferently but, after a narrow-eyed look at Cindy, who was displaying an inordinate amount of cleavage, moved off in the direction of the Broomstick's office.

"Whew!" Sid straightened up and wiped his brow. "Wouldn't like to meet her in a dark alley!"

"I don't even want to see her around here," Cindy said.

"You could always leave," Annabel tried again.

"Oh, no, we've got too much to do around here."

"Quite right—and you'd better finish with that carpet now. That's all you're going to accomplish today." *If only*, Annabel thought, *she could get another look at that other carpet, the one in Arthur Arbuthnot's office. A close look.*

"Oh, I dunno." Sid rubbed his sleeve over a large button on his shirt. "Haven't done too badly—so far."

"Sid's got the latest in spy cameras," Cindy said proudly. "No one even knows he's snapping them."

"Got a great one of the old boy in the doorway." Sid rubbed the lens again. "Looked like a stranded trout."

"You'll be the ones stranded if you're reported to the Press Council. That doorway is very identifiable. They'll have you dead to rights on flouting the privacy guidelines."

"Nobody pays any attention to those things any more," Cindy said. "They're out of date."

"Already?" Annabel was disbelieving. "But it's not that long ago that they came into force."

"Not much force there. How they going to police them? Oh, maybe we have to tiptoe around the kiddies," Sid conceded. "But this lot are old enough to look out for themselves."

"They're not doing too good a job of it." Cindy grinned maliciously. "Not when they've got a mole under their roof feeding the Spider."

Annabel tried to look suitably puzzled; as though she had no idea that Xanthippe, sitting in the midst of her web of gossip and waiting for the first tentative vibrations at the edge of the web to tell her that another victim had been enmeshed, was often referred to as the Spider. She tried to look as though she had never heard of Xanthippe at all.

Was Cindy looking at her speculatively?

"Be that as it may," Annabel said sternly, "if you don't work properly, you have no excuse for being here."

"Right! That's done!" Sid gave the carpet a final turn, heaved it upright and stood it in the indicated corner. "Now maybe you might be a bit more helpful for the money we've paid and give us something to do in one of the other rooms. Some place nearer to the action."

"Not much action around here," Cindy grumbled. "We'll have to make do with background stuff, general shots of the layout and people involved. Have it all on hand when the story breaks."

"You haven't paid *me* anything—and there is no story." Annabel was getting into her new role of double agent. Deny everything and disarm the suspicions of these two, while quietly continuing to feed whatever developed—well, most of the developments—to Xanthippe. In fact, Xanthippe was the perfect role model for aspiring double agents—

"What's that?" Cindy asked sharply.

"What's what?" Sid looked around.

"I thought I heard a cat." Cindy motioned for silence. "There it is again. Listen!"

"Oh, no!" Annabel moaned. "Oh, God, no!"

12

One of the cats must have crawled into her basket before she left the flat. Was it possible that she had not noticed the extra weight and had unknowingly carried the poor innocent back into the field of danger?

Only too possible, she decided glumly. The weight of the basket varied from day to day, depending on how many swatches and sample books she loaded into it.

But . . . surely she had filled the basket right up to the brim this morning? She recollected now that she had had to slip her flask lengthwise along the side of the basket, taking up the last iota of space. In that case . . .

The cat sounded closer now. It was coming this way. Annabel turned towards the door, forgetting that it was unwise to turn her back on her unwilling helpers. With her cold gaze elsewhere, Sid made a dash for freedom.

He collided with Tara, who was passing the doorway at that moment. Sid went sprawling on the floor,

Tara was knocked back against the wall and dropped what she had been carrying.

"Get the cat!" she shrieked. "Don't let her get away!"

But the cat wasn't going anywhere. It marched over to the prone Sid, glaring at him, and proceeded to tell him exactly what she thought of his rudeness and clumsiness.

"Sally!" Annabel gasped—and then looked again. Not quite, but a closer match than Salvatore. The world was full of tabby cats. This one was definitely female, dainty, petite, with a touch more white in her markings—and very opinionated. Her opinion of Sid was not favourable and she was letting everyone know it.

"She's got your number, all right," Cindy chuckled, looking down at the scolding cat.

"*Now* what?" The Broomstick burst out of her office and advanced upon the scene. She appeared to barely restrain herself from kicking Sid as she passed him. Annabel sympathized with her, for once. She was beginning to feel a growing desire to kick Sid herself.

"I found Sally!" Tara announced triumphantly. She scooped up the scolding cat and cuddled it. "She knew her Auntie Tara and she came to me straight away, didn't you, darling?"

The cat touched noses with her delicately and chirruped agreement. Then she looked down at Sid, who was scrambling to his feet, and added a few more comments, obviously disparaging. Annabel could not help but agree with her.

"Noisy creature!" The Broomstick radiated disapproval from every pore. "Can't it shut up for even a minute?"

The cat looked at her curiously. It was a very young cat, Annabel realized, just out of kittenhood and into feline adolescence, quite a bit younger than Sally. It was quite obviously someone's pampered pet, well-fed, well-groomed, happy and trusting, unaware that the world could present any dangers, or even problems. Annabel wondered where Tara had found her—and where her owner might be.

"She's a sassy little thing," Tara agreed. "Aren't you, Sassy? I mean, Sally! Sally!"

"Probably a bit of Siamese blood in there somewhere," Cindy said. "They talk a lot."

The Broomstick sniffed and turned to glare at Cindy. "Don't you have work to do?" she demanded. "If you've finished, you can leave the premises. We don't need workmen underfoot wasting time drinking cups of tea."

"Chance would be a fine thing," Sid complained. "I haven't seen a cup of tea all day."

"There's plenty for them to do." Kelda appeared suddenly, intent on protecting her—or, rather, their—investment.

"Yes, indeed." Annabel's grim tone let them know that their relief was premature. "They're going to wash the walls down now."

"Hold on, hold on," Sid bleated. "It's lunchtime. Time for a sandwich and a pint of beer at the pub. We're entitled to a break."

"We can send out for sandwiches," Annabel said.

If they ever got out, they might not come back—and certainly not in any state to do any work.

"I won't have them drinking in here!" the Broomstick snapped.

"I wouldn't dream of allowing it," Annabel assured her, with the complacency of one who had already arranged her own supplies. "He can have his cup of tea now."

For good measure, the cat added her opinion.

"You can just shut up!" Sid shouted at the cat, the only being who had no power to control his fate. "I've 'ad enough of you!"

"Now you've frightened her," Tara protested, cuddling the cat, who had shrunk back against her. "There was no need for that." The cat grumbled agreement.

"Quiet, now," Tara frowned. "I told you, you're all right."

The cat voiced her growing doubt.

"Doesn't that creature ever shut up?" The Broomstick glared at it.

"Don't you know?" Dangerously, Cindy caught the slip and challenged her. "I thought the cat belonged here. You ought to be used to it."

"I take care of Sally most of the time," Tara said. Annabel noticed that her hand had slipped upwards and tightened around the cat's throat, ready to choke off any more sounds. "Miss Stringer deals with the business side of things."

The explanation had a double-pronged effect, Annabel noted with reluctant appreciation: it excused the Broomstick's blunder and, at the same time, it reinforced Tara's argument that she should be given custody of the cat. Arthur Arbuthnot had intended his cat to reside with someone it could love and trust.

The cat appeared to be having second thoughts. It wriggled uneasily and twisted round to look up at Tara, as though sensing a certain lack of enthusiasm in the people around her. She began to voice a question which was—quite literally—choked off.

The cat began to struggle in earnest, alarmed by the no longer friendly pressure on her throat.

"Now stop that!" Tara's grip tightened. The cat reacted instantly and instinctively.

"OOOOOOW!" Tara dropped the cat and stared incredulously at the thin line of blood welling up from a deep scratch along her forearm. "That monster scratched me!"

The cat dashed down the hallway, uttering loud complaints of her own.

"Not all that fond of you, it seems," the Broomstick said, with her usual grim relish.

Tara shot her a venomous glance and turned away but, before she could pursue the cat, there was a triumphant shout from one of the other rooms.

"Sally! Sally's back!" Neville came into view, holding aloft the cursing, spitting, captured cat.

"Back?" Cindy and Sid were paying far too much attention—especially for a pair of itinerant decorators. "Back from where? Where's she been, then?"

"I believe you wanted your lunch." The Broomstick eyed them without favour. "I suggest you go and get it. Now!" She met Annabel's eyes and added implacably. "All of you."

Annabel knew when it was time for a strategic

withdrawal. It was obvious that the family intended a Council of War. She could probably pick up the gist of it later. Meanwhile, it would not be a bad idea to accompany Cindy and Sid and make sure that they returned to do some more work.

She made only one mistake in her calculations: she met Sassy's worried eyes before she left.

Lunch was silent and sulky; they were the quietest table in the Bower. Sid disappeared into his pint of beer. Cindy slipped away to make a series of telephone calls, huddled in a corner with her mobile phone and nibbling on a sandwich. Kelda was almost too nervous to eat for fear of imminent criticism from Annabel, who was holding her fire waiting for a more opportune—and private—moment.

The atmosphere enveloping them all was still fraught when they returned to the apartment. Except for Sid, who was exceptionally relaxed. He must have managed to get his mug refilled, perhaps more than once, without being caught; he was humming a bawdy song under his breath. Too bawdy to be reprimanded for, because one would have to admit to knowing the words. One simply had to tighten one's lips and thank heaven he wasn't hanging wallpaper this afternoon.

The apartment seemed curiously deserted. Annabel found herself listening for the sound of a cat, but there wasn't a meow or a purr to be heard. Had they silenced Sassy already? Or was she sleeping? Possibly Tara had carried the cat down to Arthur Arbuthnot's quarters, into which she appeared to have moved since her fiancé's demise, the better to establish her claim to all or part of the estate. In possession of both cat and living quarters, Tara was increasingly a force to be reckoned with.

Except that she didn't have the cat. Not the real Sally. She had an unwitting imposter, who was quite probably named Sassy, the name Tara had let slip. A good name for a talkative cat. But, most unfortunately, that talkativeness could be an irritating trait to someone who did not know or understand cats. There was every reason to suspect that Sassy's days would be numbered, once the estate was safely in her custodian's possession.

Annabel fought off a feeling of impending doom. There wasn't room in the Knightsbridge flat for another cat. There wasn't. And, even if there were, how could she take such a talkative cat into protective custody? Sassy would announce her presence every step of the way out of the building.

No, this one would just have to take her chances. How much danger could she be in at the moment? The family had to have a live cat to present to Mr. Pennyman on Monday—and had to keep it alive until the probate process was finished and the estate distributed. After that . . . ?

Uneasiness held Annabel in its grip and would not let her go; it crawled along her spine and tickled the back of her neck. She looked around restlessly, went to stand in the doorway and listened intently.

Was there a faint mewl coming from behind one of the closed doors at the end of the corridor?

"I'll be right back," she told the indifferent Cindy

and Sid. "I just want to check a few points with Dora Stringer."

Kelda gave her an anxious look, but made no reply. Cindy and Sid met each other's eyes and turned to regard Kelda with some animosity.

As Annabel moved away, she thought she caught the faint echo of ". . . our money back . . .". But that was Kelda's problem. Kelda had got herself into this and she was going to have to take the consequences.

Unusually, Dora Stringer's door was closed. Surely, she couldn't have lost all interest in what was going on outside? Or was it possible that she wanted some privacy for herself?

Gleefully, Annabel gave a perfunctory tap on the door and flung it open. "Sorry to disturb you—" she began and stopped.

The office was empty. No Broomstick caught reading a romantic novel, or painting her toenails a lurid red, or even tippling from Arthur Arbuthnot's private stock. Ah, well, these disappointments come to us all.

A flutter of wings caught her attention as a pigeon alighted on the windowsill. The window behind the desk was wide open.

Sassy!

Annabel rushed to the window, frightening the pigeon back into the sky, and leaned out, terrified of seeing the small furry body lying on the pavement below.

The body she saw was much larger.

Annabel reeled back into the room, trying to choke off a scream, not very successfully. Her high-pitched strangled wail brought the others running.

"Oh great!" Cindy and Sid shouldered her aside to lean out of the window themselves. There was a series of clicking sounds, then Sid drew back into the room.

"You do it?" He focused on Annabel, who raised her hands to shield her face. "Don't worry—she had it coming." He turned to Cindy. "Deal with this. I've got to get down there before the cops arrive."

Screams and yelps of outrage along the corridor announced that the others were arriving and that Sid was crashing into them on his way to the lift. A plaintive sustained yowl was Sassy's disapproving contribution to the proceedings.

"Don't say anything," Cindy said quickly. "I want to get their unprompted reactions. I'll interview you later. Don't talk to any other media. This is our Exclusive. We'll make it worth your while. We might even get you off."

"Don't be ridiculous!" Annabel snapped. "I didn't do it. You know there wasn't time, we've been together all day." When did it happen? How long had Dora Stringer's body lain there? It was on the quiet side of the building, around the corner from the main road. There wouldn't have been many passers-by.

"Pity. The deal could have been lucrative—for us both." Cindy lost interest in her and turned to watch as the others swarmed into the office.

Where had they all come from so suddenly? They had obviously all been together. Neville was carrying Sassy, Tara clung to his arm. Zenia and Wystan were right behind them and Luther brought up the rear with a curiously smug expression on his face. Whatever they had been plotting obviously suited him right down to the ground.

"What is it? What's the matter?" Zenia glared at the two women standing by the window. "Who was making that dreadful noise? Why?"

In the distance, there was the rising and falling shriek of an approaching siren and Annabel noticed for the first time that Kelda was missing. Had she called the police and were they arriving so soon? Her paparazzi friends wouldn't like that.

"Where's Dora?" Zenia was suddenly, sharply aware that someone else was missing. "Why isn't she here? She was supposed to be getting those figures together for—" She broke off, realizing that Cindy was gesturing towards the open window with a strange expression on her face.

Sassy gave a muted strangulated wail. Annabel saw that Neville had his thumb and forefinger circled round her muzzle, holding her mouth shut. Sassy kept trying to pull her head away, twisting and squirming.

Zenia crossed to the window and leaned out. Her face was grim when she withdrew and turned to look at the others.

"That's Dora?" It was a question without hope of a contradiction. "What happened?"

"I don't know," Annabel said. "The office was empty when I came in to ask her something. The window was open. I looked out and . . ."

Sassy gave another eerie wail.

"Too bad she didn't take that cat with her," Zenia said. She looked from the cat to the open window. A scheming look came into her eyes.

Annabel could read her thoughts as clearly as though she were speaking them: *If we could show Pennyman the cat's body and say that Dora took it with her when she jumped, they couldn't blame us for it and we'd get the estate without any more nonsense.*

The telephone on the desk bleeped suddenly, startling them all, issuing a summons for a woman who was now beyond answering it. They stared at the telephone, reluctant to touch it.

"Hello?" Unexpectedly, Wystan moved forward, a step ahead of Luther, and murmured into the phone. "I'm sorry, I'm afraid Miss Stringer isn't available at the moment. May I take a message?" He listened without expression. "I see. Yes. I'll have . . . someone . . . get back to you later." He looked shaken as he rang off, as though he had suddenly realized what he had said, as though the reality of the situation had just forced itself upon him.

When the telephone rang again, almost immediately, he made no effort to reach for it, but allowed Luther to take the call while he walked over to the window and leaned against the frame, breathing deeply.

"Right, Mark, we know," Luther said quietly. "Yes, awful. No, everyone's here. Yes," he sighed heavily. "Yes, I suppose you can send them right up when they arrive. Oh—ring through first, of course, and give us a bit of warning." He replaced the receiver slowly and looked at the others.

"Were you talking about the police?" Zenia demanded. "Has some interfering busybody called the police?" She glared directly at Annabel.

"When would I have had the time?" Annabel fought back. "I'd only just discovered the—what had happened—when you all came rushing in. You've been with me every moment since."

"None of us knew anything about it," Cindy said. "There wasn't a sound—until Annabel screamed. Someone outside must have called the cops. Somebody who saw her go out the window . . . or found her on the pavement. You can't just leave a body sprawled on the pavement."

"Indeed?" Zenia's face said that the only correct thing to do about a body sprawled on the pavement was to kick it into the gutter. None of this nonsense about ambulances and police.

"*Aaarrrrooooooeeeeoow!*" Sassy squirmed free of Neville's restraining hand and sent out a heartfelt yowl.

"Shut that beast up!" Zenia transferred her murderous gaze to the cat; another body she would like to see kicked into the gutter.

"Sorry, Mother, she's a slippery little thing. Here now—stop that. Ouch!" Neville yanked back his hand and Sassy leaped to the floor and darted down the hallway.

"Get her!" Zenia commanded. "Lock her up somewhere! There'll be strangers in and out of here this afternoon. We don't want to lose this one, too."

Too? Cindy's lifted head and narrowed eyes showed that the odd phrasing had not escaped her. Why such a fuss about the cat? There was more of a story developing here every minute.

Sassy's plaintive wail could be heard loudly, its

meaning plain: she didn't like this place, she no longer liked these people, she wanted to go home. Home—did they hear her?—home! Now!

Annabel couldn't have agreed more.

The others looked towards the sound with varying degrees of irritation. Sassy had been a popular substitute for Sally—until the moment she opened her mouth. Now she was rapidly losing every bit of popularity she had had.

"Doesn't it ever shut up?" Neville echoed his mother's complaint, frowning at the bite mark on his finger. "Do you think—?" A more pressing concern occurred to him. "Do you think I might need an anti-rabies shot? The thing bit me to the bone."

"Oh, don't be so silly!" Tara's patience snapped. "You're barely touched—she didn't even draw blood! It was just a little nip. And English cats don't have rabies! If you're afraid of her, I'll shut her in the study myself." She started off after the cat, calling, "Sa-ally . . . It's all right, Sally. Auntie Tara will take care of you."

The telephone rang again. Luther picked it up. "Already? Right. Thanks, Mark."

"They're on their way?" Neville twitched. "Up here? Now? Why?"

"They'll have questions." Luther shrugged. "Probably they'll want someone to go down and identify the body. All the customary things. A woman has died, they can't just ignore it."

"What questions?" Wystan looked to his wife unhappily. "What can we possibly tell them?"

"Poor, dear, *tragic* Dora!" Zenia swept them all

with a basilisk look, clearly issuing orders. "She always seemed so sure of herself, so efficient, so in control. How were we to know that she would feel that she could not bear to go on living without Arthur?"

13

Sally and Salvatore came running to welcome her as she turned the key in the lock, swung the door open and stepped into the Knightsbridge flat. Their little noses were working overtime, twitching and sniffing, their eyes focused on her basket, they both began to purr.

"I stopped to pick up a roast chicken," Annabel told them. "I can see I made the right choice." She hoped there was enough for all of them, but she didn't particularly care. Right now, a martini and a couple of aspirins were as much as she felt able to face.

The cats followed her into the kitchen and watched her set the basket on the table. She opened one side of the hinged lid, gently lifted out the unconscious Sassy and laid her on the table beside the basket. Both cats leaped up to investigate.

"If you wake her, you'll be sorry," Annabel warned them. "She's pretty noisy. I had to spike her milk with my martini to knock her out so that I could smuggle her out of the flat. I do hope you're all going to get along together, there's nowhere else I could take her."

Salvatore raised his head and beamed at Annabel, his affable leer becoming more affable than ever. Another pretty little female *and* a large roasted chicken. He head-butted Annabel's arm fondly. What a splendid establishment this woman ran!

Sally wasn't so sure. She circled Sassy's still form cautiously and ignored the blandishments of roast chicken. She seemed profoundly uneasy and, with every sniff at the recumbent form, she became more unsettled. She gave Annabel a questioning look.

"I wish I knew," Annabel said wearily. "I wish I knew what you want to know—and I wish I could explain it to you and be sure you understood. But right now it's all too much for me."

Hoping she wasn't being foolish in turning her back on the cats on the table, she went to the fridge to pull out the martini pitcher and pour a generous one into the chilled glass. When, after a long swallow, she turned back to the table, the situation seemed to be settling down.

Sally was industriously washing Sassy's face. Salvatore was dividing his attention between the two females and the carrier bag in which the roast chicken still reposed. He met Annabel's eyes and his loud purr rasped out hopefully.

"Yes, yes," Annabel said. "I know you must be hungry. But, if you think you've had a long day, you should have seen mine."

It had been an endless afternoon; she took another gulp of her martini. The police questioning had been repetitive and tedious. Fortunately, she and her team had been able to alibi each other, thanks to her determination not to let them out of her sight. When, at last, the police had dismissed them in order to concentrate on a determined questioning of the family, Annabel no longer had fears that her team would desert her. Their story had come alive, so to speak, with the Broomstick's death, and it would take dynamite to keep them away from the premises now.

Annabel had delayed her departure until the others had left and the police were fully occupied with the family. Then there had been the problem of getting Sassy to safety. Finding her saucer of milk and doctoring it, then standing over her while she drank it and, still mumbling, fell asleep. The harrowing long tiptoe down the hallway, hoping no door would open suddenly or that Sassy would wake and start talking again, had taken more out of her nervous system than she cared to acknowledge. The outside world had never looked so good.

Salvatore head-butted her again, a bit tetchily this time, reminding her that she was awfully slow about carving the chicken.

"Sorry," she apologized. "I was lost in thought." She wrestled with the clingfilm swathing the chicken until it gave way suddenly, smearing her hands with grease.

"Ooops!" Absently, she began licking her fingers. Salvatore thrust himself forward urgently. He might be a rough diamond, but he was a gentleman—no lady need ever lick her chicken-greasy fingers when he was around. Allow him! The rasping tickling little tongue made her laugh aloud and brightened her spirits immeasurably.

Sally abandoned the semi-comatose Sassy and strolled over to see what was going on. She found a grease blob on the table and tidied it up. Both cats, Annabel noticed, were inching their way closer to the large fragrant chicken.

"Thank you, that's enough." She pulled her hand back and gently pushed both eager heads away. "Just you wait a minute. I don't want this chicken torn apart. We'll serve it in a civilized manner."

Two heads turned towards her in injured dignity. They wouldn't dream of having it any other way. Little pink tongues swiped across anticipating lips. For an instant, sharp little fangs gleamed disconcertingly.

"Yes, yes, I'm hurrying," Annabel placated. She tried to fend off the eager cats while briskly carving off large chunks of meat. Every once in a while, she directed a slice on to her own plate; it was her supper, too.

It was amazing, the way they could eat and purr at the same time. Smiling at the two happy cats, she reached out for a nibble from her own dish and encountered a sleek little head.

"That's my plate!" she protested.

"Mmmrrumph-uumph!" Revived by the scent and taste of the succulent chicken, Sassy was not above speaking with her mouth full. *"Grrr . . ."* she added, for good measure, just in case anyone was thinking of trying to take that chicken away from her.

Sally and Salvatore looked up briefly, but returned to their meals when they saw there was not going to be a fight.

"Sorry to disappoint you," Annabel murmured,

"but there's enough for all of us. That's why I got the largest one they had."

Sassy came up for air, blinked and shook her head. Despite the chicken, she was clearly not a completely happy cat. She shook her head again, possibly it was aching.

"Bit of a hangover?" Annabel was sympathetic. "Sorry about that, but I had to keep you quiet. If they'd caught us, you'd never have got out of that house." *Not alive, that is*. Still uncertain about how much cats understood, Annabel felt it was more discreet not to worry Sassy with that unpleasant possibility.

Worry Sassy? Annabel, what are you thinking about?

On the rare occasions when her conscience surfaced, it took on the voice of her old nanny, disappointed in her and disapproving of any scheme she had in mind. *It's all very well to save the cats, but a woman died this afternoon. There was no one to save her.*

And no one would want to, Annabel answered her nanny-conscience rebelliously. But the seed had been planted.

Perhaps that's the saddest thing of all. No friends and no future, once the only employer who'd put up with her died. No wonder she chose suicide—

"NO!" Annabel said out loud. The cats looked at her askance. Nanny disappeared back into the deepest recesses of Annabel's mind, where she usually lay dormant. "NO!"

No, the Broomstick was not the sort to kill herself

just because Arthur Arbuthnot had died. Especially not since he had left her a tidy inheritance. Dora Stringer would not have to look for another employer, she could have retreated to a country cottage, gone on a trip around the world, or done whatever she wanted to do. She would not have chosen to dive out of the window.

It was Zenia who had proposed the suicide theory to the police, backed immediately by her husband and son. Even Tara had been quick to agree that a poor distraught secretary with, possibly, a secret passion for her employer, might have taken such a desperate step in a moment of temporary insanity. Luther had charitably suggested that it was equally possible that Dora might have been leaning out of the window for a breath of air—or possibly to chase the pigeons away—and overbalanced and fell. Misadventure, was his summing up of the situation.

They were all lying. Did the police realize that?

Why should they? They had no reason to connect the two deaths in any sinister manner. A man had died; his spinster secretary had committed suicide. These things happen.

Only someone who had been there from the beginning, who had been on the scene when Arthur Arbuthnot had . . . collapsed . . . was in a position to think the unthinkable.

Murder . . . double murder. Someone had stabbed Arthur Arbuthnot in the back and left him dying in his office. Someone had pushed Dora Stringer out of that window. Undoubtedly the same someone. Someone familiar, someone trusted, someone able to get close enough to the victims to . . . to make them the victims.

Kelda had not been out of her sight for more than a moment all afternoon. The thought rose to the surface of Annabel's consciousness, bringing with it a rush of relief. She now acknowledged the suspicion that had been nagging at her for days.

Kelda had rushed to administer first aid to the fallen tycoon. Kelda—who worked surrounded by the potentially deadly tools of her trade: sharp chisels, sharper knives and blades of all sizes, wallpaper shears, scissors . . .

Kelda—who hated Arthur Arbuthnot for the way he had treated Mark. It would have been so easy for her to have slipped a knife in and out of his back while she heaved his body about under the guise of trying to save his life . . .

A gentle insistent head-butting against her arm and a querulous murmur of complaint from her other side, brought Annabel back to the present. She looked down into Sally's eyes, bright, sad, old as time.

Sally had been witness to the first murder, taking the sudden opportunity to slip into the forbidden territory on the heels of the killer. A witness who could never identify or testify against the killer.

Sassy began to complain afresh, looking down at Annabel's erstwhile plate; her complaint seemed to have something to do with the fact that here was all this lovely chicken and she didn't feel well enough to finish it. She shook her head unhappily.

Salvatore was instantly at her side. Another damsel in distress—how fortunate that he was on hand to assist. He gave her a reassuring lick, lowered his head over the plate and made short work of the chicken.

Sassy did not appear to find this entirely satisfactory. She muttered something that did not sound quite ladylike, but did not seem able to take the matter further.

"Go and lie down," Annabel advised her. "Sleep it off and you'll feel a lot better."

It was Sally who was the first to yawn, give herself a quick wash of paws and face—just a lick and a promise, really—and curl up into a soft purring ball of fur.

Salvatore cleaned every plate and looked around hopefully.

Sassy voiced one final tirade, but her heart wasn't in it. Flicking her ears and muttering uneasily, she hunched down, tucked her tail tightly around her body and closed her eyes. Even so, the discontented muttering continued.

Annabel had absently begun pulling shreds of meat off the chicken carcase and nibbling them as she observed the cats. Now, as she paused with a chunk of chicken just torn off, she felt a gentle tug and looked down to find Salvatore pulling at the other end of the chunk.

"It *is* good, isn't it?" She relinquished it to him and bemusedly pulled off another chunk which, somehow or other, he also got. His deep throbbing purr encouraged her to spoil him. She gave him another chunk and then another.

"This is the last one," she said finally. "I can't stand here and hand-feed you all night."

He didn't see why not. He rubbed his head along her hand coaxingly and she softened.

"Well, perhaps just one—"

The doorbell pealed sharply.

Annabel froze. Who on earth—? She wasn't expecting anyone. She didn't want to see anyone. Some stranger must have pressed the wrong button by mistake.

Annabel ambled over to the closed-circuit-TV screen above the entryphone and was horrified to see Tara waving frantically at the camera. She recoiled as though Tara could also see her. The doorbell rang again, Tara began exaggeratedly mouthing something at the camera. Sassy lifted her head and gave an unhappy little mew.

She couldn't let anyone in here! Annabel stared unbelievingly at the screen as one of the other residents came along, inserted his key in the lock and stepped back, beaming, to allow Tara to precede him into the entrance hall. Men! There were notices on every floor warning residents that they should not admit anyone into the building who was not known to them personally. It seemed a pretty face was introduction enough. If burglars came in pairs of pretty females, some men would undoubtedly help them carry their loot down the stairs and hold the car door open for them.

Meanwhile, Tara was on her way up. Was it possible to pretend she wasn't home? Too late, Annabel realized that she had not drawn the curtains. Tara would have seen the lights and known that she was here.

Annabel gathered up the startled cats and bundled them into the bedroom, tossing them on the bed. Sassy raised her voice in protest and Annabel hastily rearranged them: Sassy on the bottom of the pile, the other two on top of her.

"Keep her quiet," she pleaded, and tossed the quilt over them as a further muffling measure. She closed the door firmly behind her, wishing that it had a lock, and also that there was not an inch gap at the bottom where the carpet had flattened down. How much sound could escape through that?

The inner doorbell shrilled. Annabel caught up the cats' dishes and dumped them in the sink, then advanced slowly towards the door, looking around. Was there anything else that might give the game away?

"Annabel! Annabel!" The doorbell and then a persistent knocking reinforced the call. "Annabel! I know you're in there! It's me, Tara. Let me in!"

Were the cat hairs terribly noticeable? Possibly not to someone who was not looking for them. But what about the frayed material at the end of the sofa where someone had sharpened little claws too enthusiastically? Again, possibly not—unless to eyes searching for evidence.

"Annabel! Annabel!" The voice sharpened imperiously. "I *must* talk to you. Let me in!" The bell rang again, the knocking intensified and an indignant muffled howl sounded from the bedroom. This was no place for a cat with a hangover.

"Just a minute—" Annabel called. "I'm coming!" Desperate measures were needed. She flew into the kitchen, sloshed some milk into a saucer and recklessly added gin. The cats looked up expectantly as she entered the bedroom.

"Here!" She set the saucer on the floor beside the bed, caught up Sassy and put her on the floor beside the saucer, dunking her nose into the potent contents. "Hair of the dog—if you'll pardon the expression." She paused to make sure that Sassy was lapping it; with any luck, it would put her back to sleep. Sally and Salvatore leaped to the floor and began circling the saucer with interest, ever alert for new gourmet experiences.

Annabel closed the bedroom door firmly again, shook herself, and gave a final sweeping glance around the sitting room.

"Annabel! Are you all right?"

"Sorry." Annabel crossed and opened the door with an innocent expression. "I'm afraid you caught me in the loo."

"Oh!" It was the only explanation that was both acceptable and too awkward to pursue. "I'm sorry. I should have—I mean, how was I to—Er, sorry." Thoroughly wrong-footed, Tara advanced into the sitting room and changed the subject. "How charming."

"Yes, isn't it? Not quite my taste but"—Annabel played her trump card—"I'm subletting from Lady Cosgreave so, of course, I can't change anything. Dinah is so sensitive."

"Of course," Tara agreed cordially. Her cool assessing gaze swept the room and dismissed everything in it. "You would have done it up so much better."

"I'd like to think so," Annabel murmured modestly, wondering just what Tara was up to. At least she did not appear to be in search of missing felines; despite her words, she was showing no real interest in her surroundings.

"Oh, but you would!" Tara gazed earnestly into Annabel's face. "You're so clever—and so talented. I can't wait to see Arthur's pokey old apartment when you've finished with it."

"How kind of you to say so." Annabel had always been wary of flattery and this was being laid on with the proverbial trowel.

"No, no, you deserve it. You've already done wonders with the place." Uninvited, Tara sank down in a corner of the sofa and placed her handbag beside her feet, clearly settling in for a long stay.

Already listening for any betraying sounds from behind the bedroom door, Annabel discovered a new worry: the catnip mouse the cats had been playing with was lying temporarily abandoned between the sofa leg and Tara's handbag. The instant Tara looked down, she would discover it.

"How about a drink?" Annabel asked urgently. "What would you like?"

"Why, thank you." Tara seemed a bit startled at the fervency of the invitation. "Whatever you're having will be fine."

"Martinis," Annabel said firmly, adding, "I make them rather strong, I'm afraid."

"I don't think I'll mind that." Tara gave a little shudder and leaned back against the cushions. "This has been quite a day."

"It certainly has," Annabel agreed. "Why don't you just close your eyes and rest a moment? I'll be right back with the drinks." She waited until Tara had obediently closed her eyes before going into the kitchen. With any luck, Tara wouldn't move for a few minutes, she looked completely exhausted. That must have been quite a session with the police. But why should Tara come to see her right now? Surely, anything could have waited until morning.

There was one generous measure left in the pitcher. Annabel poured it for Tara and filled her own glass with water. This might be a moment when she needed all her wits about her.

"Here we are." As she handed the drink to Tara, she gave the catnip mouse a brisk kick. But she misjudged the force of her kick and saw the mouse go skittering under the sofa and come out the other side. She heard the faint thump as it hit the bedroom door.

"Oh, thank you." Tara took a sip and shuddered. "Delicious," she lied. "Umm, do you think I might have a bit of ice in it?"

"I'll get some." Annabel was used to this reaction, practically everyone she knew insisted on watering down their drinks; at least, they did when she had mixed them. "Wimps" was the word that sprang to mind.

Although perhaps Tara shouldn't be included in that category. Despite her request, the level of liquid in her glass had descended noticeably when Annabel returned immediately with two ice cubes in another glass.

"Oh, thank you." Tara seemed surprised when Annabel tipped them into her glass, perhaps she had forgotten her request. "Actually, this, um, rather grows on one the way it is."

"I've always found that," Annabel agreed absently, wondering how long Tara intended keeping up the social chitchat before coming to the point.

Tara appeared to be in no hurry. She looked around the room again, more carefully this time, and Annabel flinched as her gaze rested on the shredded upholstery on the arm of the wing chair, where sharp little claws had been sharpened even more. She would have to do something about that before Dinah returned and saw it.

And hadn't Dinah muttered something about no pets being allowed under the terms of her lease or Dinah would risk forfeiting the lease? It didn't bear thinking about and Annabel tried to put it out of her mind.

"What did the police have to say?" Annabel attempted to jolt Tara out of the trance she seemed to have fallen into.

"Police?" Tara looked so vague she might never have heard of such an organization.

"Police," Annabel insisted. "You know. All those strange people in dark-blue uniforms who were milling around the place when I left."

"Oh. Yes." Tara took another sip. "The police. They were really very understanding . . . eventually. These things happen. They must see so much of them, poor dears. A terrible job, really, but they've gone now. I think they're satisfied. They haven't sealed up any of the rooms, or anything. That was what I wanted to tell you. It's all right to come back to work as usual in the morning."

"Is it?" Annabel looked at her coldly. That message could quite easily have been conveyed over the telephone. "It may have escaped your attention, but tomorrow is Saturday."

"Exactly! That's why I wanted to see you tonight." Tara faced her triumphantly. "Saturday is when you designers trawl the street markets for all your exciting finds, isn't it? Oh"—she cut off any protest Annabel might be about to make—"I know you have your favourite suppliers and they give you special discounts and all that, but the real profit is in the little things you can pick up in street markets and junk shops, isn't it?"

Annabel opened her mouth, but nothing came out. She was beginning to feel a bit dizzy.

"So I thought you might be willing to let me trail along with you tomorrow—" Tara finally got around to the purpose of her visit. "I'll be very quiet and won't interfere with your bargaining. I'll just listen and learn. And, maybe, you could indicate some of the things you want for the flat and I could buy them myself—and resell them to you later." She paused and watched Annabel intently to see how she would respond to this proposal.

"At a profit, I presume." Annabel found her voice, although it was a weak one. She had never had any intention of trawling street markets or bargaining with suppliers; she had planned to leave all that to Kelda.

"Naturally," Tara said expectantly. "You can't tell me it isn't done all the time. One of my friends collected a nice little nest egg from the interior designer when her husband had his offices completely renovated. There's nothing wrong with it, it's just business."

"Er . . . quite," Annabel agreed cautiously, her stunned mind trying to cope with this unexpected development. "The only thing is"—she extemporized wildly—"I'm going away for the weekend. Visiting friends in the country. Early train in the morning. I won't be doing any shopping at all, just relaxing and unwinding. Perhaps we could do something Monday."

"But the best street markets are on weekends," Tara protested. "Besides, there's the appointment with Mr. Pennyman on Monday. He wants to meet the cat."

The cats! Annabel had forgotten them completely. Automatically, she checked the bedroom door—and froze in horror.

The door was still closed, but a little dappled brown paw had snaked out beneath it and was raking the carpet, trying to capture its catnip mouse. If Tara turned around and saw that—

"Perhaps Tuesday, then?" Annabel offered, watching a tiny claw connect with the mouse's nose and then pull the toy sharply up against the door. Surely it was her imagination that the toy made a soft thud as it hit the door?

"Tuesday . . ." Tara mused. "That's really not very satisfactory.

Abruptly, Annabel realized that, depending on the decision of Mr. Pennyman and the responses of the family, Tara might no longer be part of the entourage on Tuesday. There was an underlying suspicion that she certainly wouldn't be if Zenia had anything to do with it. If she was unacceptable as a spouse for Zenia's nephew, she was twice as unacceptable as a future daughter-in-law. Perhaps Tara couldn't be blamed for attempting to feather whatever nest she still possessed.

"Oh, dear." Tara gave a deep sigh. Suddenly she looked small and forlorn. "I *had* hoped we could come to some arrangement." She set down her glass and leaned forward to pick up her handbag. In another moment, she would stand and turn to face the door— the bedroom door, as well as the door to the foyer.

The telephone shrilled suddenly, startling them both. Even the little paw was withdrawn quickly, abandoning the catnip mouse to its fate. There was a waiting silence, broken only by the persistent ringing of the telephone. Instinctively, Annabel felt that it boded no good.

"I don't suppose it could be for me," Tara prodded delicately. "Although I did mention that I might drop in on you ..."

Trapped, Annabel crossed to the telephone and lifted the receiver. "Hello?"

"It's about time!" Xanthippe's strident tones set her ears ringing. "What the hell are you playing at? Why haven't you called me? Why haven't—"

"Sorry, wrong number." Annabel broke the connection, but did not replace the receiver; she set it down beside the cradle and turned back to Tara. "Wrong number."

"Oh?" Tara raised an eyebrow. "How tedious for

you." She looked at the unreplaced receiver. "Do you get many of them?"

"Too many," Annabel said promptly. "Once they start, they keep coming. Wires crossed, or something. The only thing to do is to put the phone out of action for an hour or so. That discourages them."

"I see." Tara looked as though she were seeing a manifestation of some hitherto unrecorded eccentricity.

Behind her, the little paw slid out from under the door again and began groping for its catnip mouse.

"Look—" Annabel said desperately. "Suppose I ring my friends and tell them I'll catch an afternoon train? That will give us the morning. We can do Camden Passage and perhaps Portobello Road."

"Oh, wonderful!" Tara's face cleared.

"It will mean an early start," Annabel warned. "I'll meet you at the Angel tube station at seven a.m. Outside, if it's a fine day; inside, if it's raining."

"Seven?" Tara gasped.

"And that's a bit late." Looking beyond Tara, Annabel saw a second brown paw appear beneath the bedroom door, at such an angle that it had to be another cat joining in the game. And was that a faintly complaining mew in the background? "The dealers all get there at the crack of dawn."

"I suppose they do." Tara's eyelids flickered—had she heard that mew?

"Sorry." Annabel cleared her throat, giving a credible imitation of a cat's cry, and remained standing. "Well, you'll want an early night, if you have to get up so early in the morning," she hinted strongly.

"Yes. Yes, you're right. I must be going." Tara stood and seemed to hesitate.

"Yes, you must. I mean, such an early start. Sorry, but it can't be helped." Annabel closed in behind her, preventing her from turning around, and herded her towards the door.

As Tara moved ahead, Annabel saw the cluster of brown cat hairs clinging to the fawn silk skirt. Too late, Annabel remembered that Salvatore loved to curl up in the corner where Tara had been sitting.

Annabel stretched out a hand—and withdrew it quickly. To brush off the hairs would be to call attention to them. She could only hope that they fell off on Tara's way home. Or that Tara would assume that she had picked them up somewhere in the Regent's Park flat, where Sally had resided long enough to leave little souvenirs of her presence.

"I'll see you in the morning," Tara said, as Annabel opened the door for her. "The Angel at seven."

"That's right! Good night!" Annabel did not care if she seemed to slam the door upon her departing guest with undue haste. She leaned against it limply for a moment, then pushed herself away and headed for the kitchen and a well-earned martini.

14

Annabel might have been able to ignore the alarm clock in the morning—the temptation was strong—but she could not ignore the cats. Salvatore immediately prowled over to investigate the thing making strange noises which suggested something birdlike and edible might be hiding inside and promptly knocked it to the floor where it continued to tweetle. Sassy raised her head and began a dialogue with the strange object, scolding and berating it and finally dropping to the floor to join Salvatore as he began batting it about.

Only Sally seemed to feel that it was all too much effort; she snuggled closer to Annabel and went back to sleep.

"Sorry," Annabel said, dislodging her, "but I'm afraid it's time to rise and shine—for me, at any rate." Sally gave a perfunctory purr and rolled into the warm hollow left by Annabel's body. The other cats followed Annabel into the kitchen.

Sally had come a long way from the alley, Annabel reflected, glancing back at the sleeping cat, now serenely confident that there would always be food available with no need to rush and compete with the other cats for it.

Salvatore, on the other hand, was still new enough to the experience to be enchanted by it. He hurled himself against Annabel's legs, twining in and out around her ankles, purring loudly as she filled his food dish. Breakfast! And he had had dinner last night! What a world of luxury this was! And he was thriving on it, Annabel noticed, his coat was smoother and shinier, his eyes brighter, even his little snaggle-fang seemed whiter and not quite so protruding. No doubt about it, Salvatore was flourishing.

Sassy advanced to her own dish and examined it critically, then voiced a complaint. She sniffed at it, which brought further dissatisfaction. She looked at Annabel accusingly and made a few pointed comments. When nothing happened, she reluctantly sampled the offering, then launched into a tirade.

"I'm sorry, I know it's not what you're used to—but I don't know what that is." Annabel stooped to caress the indignant little creature. "I wish I did."

Sassy leaned into the caress for a moment, closing her eyes briefly, then opening them again and looking up. She let out a small wail of distress as she saw Annabel's face rather than the loved one she wanted.

"I know, I know," Annabel soothed. "You're someone's darling pet and you miss her—and she must be frantic wondering what's happened to you. Damn that selfish Tara—"

Tara! She had nearly forgotten that she was supposed to be meeting Tara and it was quarter to seven already. She'd have to skip her own breakfast, but she could pick up the No. 19 bus in Sloane Street and it would carry her direct to the Angel. The route went through the heart of the West End but, at this hour of the morning, there shouldn't be much traffic. With luck, she wouldn't be terribly late and, if there were any delays, Tara would just have to wait. Serve her right if she did. Too bad it wasn't pouring.

Annabel looked sadly at the forlorn little feline, callously catnapped to serve Tara's selfish ends. The other two cats had been waifs and strays, but such a pretty and rather spoiled little madam would never have been allowed to stray far from her doting owner. Tara had probably picked her up in the Regent's Park area, perhaps even lifted her off her own doorstep.

"Mmmrr . . . rrreoow . . ." Sassy gave herself a little shake and slowly began to nibble at her unsatisfactory breakfast, still mumbling complaints.

"I'll do my best to get you home," Annabel promised her.

Tara was waiting behind the glass entrance of the tube station, although it wasn't actually raining, just grey and a bit misty. She had the anxious expression and large empty shopping bag of the hopeful bargain-hunter.

Annabel relaxed a little. Perhaps Tara was genuinely intent on exploring the possibilities of earning something extra on the side, or perhaps even looking into a new career as an interior designer.

Or possibly—a more disquieting thought came to Annabel—Tara was the killer and wished to find out how much Annabel knew or suspected about the recent deadly events she had, if not quite witnessed, been in close conjunction to.

That new suspicion made for a slightly less than auspicious start to their expedition.

"We turn along here," Annabel directed, neatly sidestepping so that Tara was beside her rather than a couple of steps behind her. She realized that she did not want to turn her back on anyone from the highly suspect group that had surrounded Arthur Arbuthnot.

Idiot! Idiot! Annabel silently berated herself. She had been so caught up in rescuing the cats that she had allowed herself to keep forgetting that there was a sinister reason for their plight. It was highly unlikely that the deaths of Arthur Arbuthnot and Dora Stringer had been accidental; even less likely that they were unconnected. Someone had been responsible—and that someone might be here with her right now, watching for an opportunity to make her the third victim.

Had she carelessly condemned herself to a jolly morning's shopping with a murderess?

The first wave of early-risers were thronging the passageways, bright and alert for bargains. Surely she was safe in the midst of such a crowd. Only . . . their attention was centred on the stalls and all the enticing wares on display. They weren't wasting any attention on the passing throng—they *were* the passing throng and, after they had passed, a body could be found lying in a dark corner and no one would have noticed a thing.

Except, Annabel cheered up slightly, for the stallholders. They were keeping sharp eyes on everyone, alert to the ever-present threat from shoplifters. While they smiled and chatted with prospective customers, they watched the people beside and behind their punter. It was the oldest trick in the trade to distract a stallholder with the prospect of a large sale while a cohort quietly lifted valuables from the other end of the stall. No, they would be keeping watch; they would see and register any sinister movements or strange behaviour.

Of course, by the time they got out from behind the stall and into the passageway, a person could be dead. It didn't take long to shoot a gun or wield a knife—and the shock of witnessing such an event held spectators motionless in shock for seconds, long seconds during which a killer could escape. And it was well known that subsequent descriptions never agreed.

"Over here!" Tara had no qualms about turning her back to Annabel. She wormed her way between a group of French tourists and a gaggle of Italian tourists to stand transfixed before a window full of ornate items of furniture. "Look at that! Isn't it divine?"

Unsure of what she was being called upon to admire, Annabel gazed without enthusiasm at the entire display. "Ummm," she said noncommittally.

"Oh, yes." Tara nodded wisely, interpreting her response. "One should never seem too interested, should one?"

"You're learning," Annabel said, quite as though it had been her intention to teach that lesson. She could now see that Tara's admiring gaze was fixed on a large glass-and-inlaid-wood cabinet at the back of the window.

"Don't you think," self-preservation compelled her to add, "that it would be better to concentrate on small, easily portable objects today? We can always come back for the big stuff later."

"Oh . . . I suppose you're right," Tara agreed reluctantly.

"I am." Annabel nudged her away from the window and the tempting—but enormous—items with relief. If this whole thing fell through—as well it might, depending on what happened on Monday—she did not wish to be left with an oversize, overexpensive Edwardian cabinet on her hands.

"What about"—Tara brightened—"jewellery?"

"Small enough," Annabel agreed. "Portable enough, but . . ." She dashed Tara's hopes. "A bit hard to justify as *objets d'art* for an apartment, wouldn't you say? More for personal adornment only, although I have seen some earrings big enough to use as curtain pulls."

"Yes . . ." Tara relinquished the idea with a sigh and allowed herself to be led over to a stall piled with bobbles, bibelots and small statues.

This time Tara was unenthusiastic, while Annabel pounced on a spray of wooden roses, carved in full bloom and gilded. If they proved unsuitable for the flat, she could always give them to Dinah. The price was right, too; so right that she was afraid to haggle, in case it had been mispriced. Perhaps it had fallen off a lorry, part of the spoils of a burglary. That was always a hazard of street markets. However . . .

Several stalls later, Annabel was just getting into her stride when Tara caved in.

"Can't we stop and have a cup of coffee?" Tara's voice took on a fretful note. "I didn't have any breakfast. We had to meet so early, there wasn't time."

"I suppose we can take a few minutes out." Annabel was glad that Tara had raised the subject first. Her own stomach had been complaining softly for some time. "That looks rather a jolly café over there."

Annabel managed to acquire one of the sidewalk tables by dint of shamelessly staking out a young couple who were nearly finished and standing beside their table, staring at every mouthful they consumed. In no time at all, they had hurriedly choked down the last bit of croissant, gulped a final mouthful of coffee and departed hastily.

"That's better." Annabel sank down into a chair that was still warm and pushed the dirty crockery to one side of the table as a strong indication to the waitress that the present occupants had not been the ones to dirty them. She looked around with approval, she really ought to do this more often. Perhaps, if she carried on with this interior-decorating lark, she would.

The pavements were thronged with happy, jostling crowds, all enjoying the mild weather and the vast array of goods on display. Local people and tourists, young and old and—

Annabel twisted around in her chair, caught by a movement at the edge of her vision. A wheelchair. Of course, there would be wheelchair-users among the crowd—and a good thing, too. As many places as

possible had wheelchair access these days, but the
pavements were still the most accessible of all. But
... wasn't there something disquietingly familiar
about that barely glimpsed figure in that wheelchair?
And why had he disappeared so quickly when she
turned?

Tara had begun rummaging in her shopping bag,
trying to rearrange the bulky and knobbly objects she
had been buying so enthusiastically, caught up in the
Saturday-morning madness that can be contagious in
street markets.

"Oh, dear," Tara said. "I hope I don't need another
bag." She pulled out a silver candelabra, already sliding free of its newspaper wrapping, twisted the paper
tighter and slid it upright along the side of the bag.

"Much better to keep to one bag," Annabel agreed.
"Lumber yourself with too many bags to carry and
you risk losing some." She watched Tara's frantic efforts to arrange everything more compactly with a
pleasant feeling of complacency. She had managed to
avoid buying anything but the carved roses herself,
while scoring Brownie points because Tara assumed
that she was holding back on the bargains to give Tara
a chance.

"Damn!" Tara pulled a brass Art-Nouveau picture
frame from the depths of the shopping bag, dislodging
other parcels on its way. Tara pushed them back frantically, not noticing that a pale blue strip of suede was
still caught in a protruding curlicue. Tara stuffed
everything down indiscriminately, looking exhausted
and uncomfortable, grimacing as she noticed that her

hands were grimy and streaked with black where the newsprint had rubbed off on them.

"The ladies' room is inside at the back," Annabel told her helpfully. "I spotted it while we were waiting for the table."

"You're sure you wouldn't like to go along first?" Tara offered anxiously as the waitress bore down on them.

"I'll stay and watch the shopping and order for you. Coffee? And those Danish pastries look awfully good."

"Would you?" Tara was properly grateful. "Coffee and Danish would be fine. Thanks so much."

"Not at all." Annabel waved her away, trying to look benevolent and not as though she had no intention of risking her unguarded cup of coffee in any proximity to dear Tara who, so far as she was concerned, was guilty until proved innocent.

Annabel gave their orders and the waitress departed briskly. And while she was thinking about things being unguarded . . . Annabel glanced around casually to make sure that she was unobserved, then, even more casually, leaned over and peered into Tara's shopping bag.

Yes, there along the side was the thin, pale-blue suede strip she had noticed earlier. A curious item for Tara to be carrying around but, equally, something that could have easily been overlooked in the stress of coping with more urgent considerations.

Annabel slid her hand down into the shopping bag and snaffled the blue suede band, coiling it neatly into her palm before withdrawing her hand.

She was just in time. When she looked up, both Tara and the waitress bearing a tray with their order were converging on the table. She opened her handbag and thrust the band into its depths—no time to investigate her prize. (She hoped it wasn't just a discarded Alice band, but surely Tara's head was bigger than that.) She pulled out a handkerchief and blew her nose loudly, then looked up with a feigned start of surprise.

"That was quick!" She pushed her handkerchief back into the handbag, hiding her ill-gotten gain with it.

"Was it?" Tara smiled vaguely and resumed her seat. The waitress set coffee and Danish before them and bustled off to another table.

"Mmm . . ." Tara wasted no time in taking a sip of her coffee and sinking gleaming white teeth—which suddenly seemed a bit fanglike—into the luscious apricot-topped pastry. "I needed this."

"You're sure you're not getting overtired?" Annabel asked solicitously. "You're looking a bit pale." She knew she was on a safe wicket there. Even in this day and age, no young woman minded being thought pale and, by implication, interesting.

"I *am* a bit tired," Tara admitted. "I haven't been sleeping well lately. So much has been happening. So much to worry about . . ."

"A very upsetting time," Annabel sympathized. "Two deaths, coming so close together. And," she added slyly, "the police involved now. There'll have to be an inquest on Miss Stringer, I suppose. Too awkward for you all."

"That woman was nothing but trouble!" Tara snapped. "It's just like her to kill herself in a way that leaves everybody with more problems than ever. Why couldn't she have just gone off and jumped into the Thames, if she had to do any jumping?"

"It could have been an accident," Annabel pointed out. "As Luther said, she might have leaned out of the window for some reason and overbalanced." Annabel carefully refrained from any mention of the word "pushed"—in her opinion, a more likely explanation.

"Oh, what does it matter?" Tara slumped in her chair. "She's dead—and she took a lot of the secrets of Arthur's business with her. There are probably some foreign accounts we'll never be able to trace now. Luther was training up well, but he still had a lot to learn."

"Actually, I was thinking more of the emotional toll on all of you," Annabel said. "I was just working there and I've found it fairly shattering. But you knew these people personally. It must be—"

"Arthur, yes." Tara's eyes clouded briefly. "Oh, I know what people think—and it's true it wasn't a great wild romance like first love or, even, infatuation—but we had something going and it might—" Tara broke off and her face hardened.

"Anyway, that's finished," she said bitterly. "And I'm not going to pretend I was devastated by Dora Stringer's death. It's too bad, of course, but she never liked me or approved of me, so you can't expect me to care about her. If she had been able to, she would have ruined everything between Arthur and me."

Annabel nodded. That had been the way she summed up the situation, too.

"If only that bitch had died first—and Arthur not at all!" Tara slammed her cup down into its saucer. "It would have made all the difference!"

This was so manifestly true from Tara's point of view that, with that plaintive cry, she removed herself from Annabel's list of possible killers.

If Tara had been going to kill anyone, she would have chosen Dora Stringer, and possibly Zenia, thus clearing away the main opposition to her marriage to Arthur Arbuthnot. And he, most certainly, would still be alive.

Poor Tara. Everything had been within her grasp—and then had been abruptly snatched away. Annabel decided that she now even forgave Tara for her treatment of Sassy. The cat hadn't been harmed, after all, and the poor woman couldn't be blamed for trying to hold on to what had almost been hers.

"Well." Annabel drained her cup and set it down. "Shall we return to the fray? Do you want to carry on here or would you like to sample Portobello Road?"

"This has been so kind of you—" Tara darted a shrewd glance through half-closed eyelids. "And it's fascinating. But—what about you? I know you have a train to catch."

So Tara was just as anxious to get rid of her as she was to see the last of Tara. Good. That simplified matters.

"Actually"—Annabel glanced at her watch—"if we were to pack it in now, I could get an earlier train."

"Of course," Tara agreed warmly. "I have a few

other things to do myself. Tomorrow is going to be a Hell Day."

Equally relieved, they beamed false smiles at each other and looked around for the waitress.

"Amazing, the way they disappear when you want them," Annabel said.

"Never mind. We'll just leave the money on the table." Tara reached into her bag and brought out a multicompartmented billfold. "Let me do it. You've been so kind, showing me the ropes."

"There!" A sudden flicker of movement at the edge of the pavement caught Annabel's attention. "Did you see that?"

"What? Where?" Distracted, Tara turned to look in the direction of Annabel's pointing finger. "I don't see anything." Automatically, she dropped a banknote beside her coffee cup.

"They might accept that here"—Annabel looked at the money—"but I doubt if you'd get a good rate of exchange for it."

"Oh!" Tara hastily snatched up the American twenty-dollar bill she had tossed down. "Wrong compartment! I haven't had a chance to get to a bank and cash in my currency left over from Mustique. Things have been so frantic!" She replaced the bill with a ten-pound note and seemed ready to rush off.

Fortunately, the waitress arrived to give her change and they departed to wave down the nearest taxi.

"Your train—" Tara said.

"No, no. You take this one," Annabel said expansively. "I'll get the next one. There's no shortage of taxis here on a Saturday morning."

"Well, if you're sure . . ." Tara murmured, diving into the taxi before Annabel could change her mind.

"Positive!" Annabel slammed the door on Tara and stepped back with a sense of freedom sweeping over her. She did not have to catch a mythical train, the rest of the day was her own. She stepped back from the kerb, waving until Tara's taxi was out of sight, and breathed a deep sigh of relief.

The relief was momentary. A disruptive movement of the crowds thronging the pavement made her turn. The stream of pedestrians was parting to allow passage to a wheelchair, then closing in again behind it.

But not so swiftly that she hadn't caught a glimpse of its occupant.

As she had suspected earlier, it was Mark. His departure told her that it had been Tara he was following. Now that Tara was gone, he had no interest in anything Annabel might do.

What *was* Mark's interest in Tara? Was it his own idea to follow her or had he been instructed to do it? Perhaps by Zenia, or even Neville, both of whom had good reason to mistrust her.

Annabel shuddered suddenly and was caught by a faint sense of panic. What was she standing here for? She had wasted enough time this morning, she ought to be home feeding the cats.

15

There was a long jagged scratch on the outside of the door to the flat and flakes of paint were missing, as though someone had tried to force entrance during her absence.

Annabel blessed the sense of alarm that had sent her hurrying back to check that the cats were safe. So immediate had been the sense of peril that she had taken a taxi after all.

The door was still firmly closed and there was silence on the other side of it. As she tried to insert the key in the lock, she saw small bright scratches around the keyhole where someone had obviously tried his or her luck with the keys they already possessed before getting down to trying brute force.

Had she disturbed the intruder at work? There had been a sense of disturbance in the air when she arrived. She had not bothered to muffle her footsteps and there had been a faint echo from the far end of the corridor by the emergency staircase. Had she heard, or had she imagined, the whisper of the fire door closing?

It was a battle to force the key into the damaged lock. Annabel had nearly despaired when, abruptly, the lock yielded and the doors swung open . . . into an empty foyer.

"Sally . . . ? Sally . . . ?" Annabel called. From the back of her mind rose the vision of Luther tiptoeing amongst the dustbins, also calling. "Salvatore . . . ? Sassy . . . ? Sally . . . ?" Automatically, she slammed the door shut behind her and fastened the safety chain. When she turned back, all three cats were lined up watching her with interest.

"Oh, thank heavens! You're all right?"

As though to reassure her, they crowded forward to mob her ankles. There was a brief pleasant interlude before Sassy began to complain again. Salvatore flicked his ears and hunched his shoulders, acquiring the look of a henpecked male who has heard it all before and is damned if he'll listen to it again. Sally gave Sassy an impatient look and moved off towards the kitchen.

Sassy mumbled several comments at them under her breath, then looked up at Annabel and emitted a long plaintive yowl.

"All right, all right." Annabel bent and scooped her up, carried her into the drawing room and settled down in a corner of the sofa. "I think I have something here that belongs to you," she told Sassy, opening her handbag.

Sassy went into hysterics at the sight of the pale-blue suede collar with the name SASSY in tiny brilliants. She flung herself at it, pawed at it, and tried to get her head into it, even though it wasn't buckled into a circle, all the while chattering wildly.

"That's what I thought," Annabel said. "In fact, I was pretty certain. Just a minute—" She tried to restrain the overexcited Sassy while she reached for the telephone.

The other two cats wandered back to see what was going on, the new pitch in Sassy's voice evidently alerting them. They watched with interest as Annabel fended off Sassy while dialling the number engraved on the little silver disc attached to the collar.

"Hello?" A woman's voice answered on the third ring. "Hello?"

"*Mmmmrrreeeeooow . . .*" Sassy heard the beloved voice and tried to climb into the telephone.

"I have someone here who'd like to speak to you," Annabel announced, somewhat unnecessarily, as Sassy was already making herself quite clear on that point. She not only wanted to speak, she wanted to go home.

"Sassy! Sassy!" the voice screamed joyfully. "Where are you?"

"Knightsbridge, actually." Annabel won possession of the phone again. "She's perfectly safe and well, but homesick."

"Knightsbridge?" The voice was startled. "How did she get way over there? We live in Regent's Park."

"Who knows?" Annabel was not going to admit that she did. "Perhaps she got into a car or on a bus and wound up over here."

"Where? Where is here?" The woman was insistent. "What's your address? I'll come and collect her immediately. In fact, I was offering a reward—"

"Not necessary," Annabel broke in. "I'm only too glad to restore her to her proper owner. I'm sorry I couldn't do it sooner, but she got separated from her collar and it was only by sheer luck that I found it." She gave the woman her address.

"Please let me speak to Sassy again," the woman said.

"Certainly." Feeling slightly foolish, Annabel held the telephone to Sassy's ear.

"Darling," the woman trilled. "Mummy's coming right away. Be a good girl and stay where you are. Mummy will be there as fast as she can."

Sassy responded with excited chirrups and purrs. She seemed to understand what had been said. She marched over to the door and sat down expectantly, still chirruping.

"Well." Annabel looked down at Sassy thoughtfully. "That's your problem solved. Now what do I do with the rest of you?"

The telephone rang, startling them all. Sassy leaped up and pranced over to the table, chattering with renewed hope. Annabel looked at the telephone uneasily, debating the wisdom of answering it. There was no one she wished to talk to right now. Why not just let it ring?

Because Sassy would not allow it, that's why. She began berating Annabel for her slowness in answering. After all, it might be for her.

She could be right. Annabel picked up the phone before remembering that she had given the woman her address but not her telephone number. "Hello . . . ?"

There was silence at the other end of the line.

"Hello . . . ? Hello . . . ?" Was that a faint uneven breathing she could hear? "Hello . . . ?"

Sassy shoved closer and added a few comments of her own. Annabel hastily covered the mouthpiece with her hand and pushed the cat away.

There was a final explosive breath—almost a snort—at the other end and the click of the receiver being replaced, then the dial tone. Annabel replaced her own receiver more slowly.

Wrong number? Heavy breather? Or something more sinister? The interrupted prowler calling to see if the coast was clear and he could return to make another attempt at forcing entry?

Had Sassy's voice carried over the line and thrown the other person off stride? Or told them what they really wanted to know? Annabel looked at Sally and Salvatore with renewed favour. Thank heaven for cats who could keep their mouths shut.

Annabel was under no illusions as to why anyone would want to break into the flat. Obviously, she hadn't been so clever as she'd thought—or the others hadn't been so stupid. Someone had recollected her ever-present basket and connected it with one—if not all—of the missing cats.

Who—or rather, which faction—was stalking her?

Had Tara been detailed to lure her out of the flat so that Neville could try to repossess Sally? Or had Mark learned that they were doing the street markets this morning and kept them under observation so that Kelda could attempt a raid on the flat?

The clumsy try, leaving a damaged lock and all those scratches on the paint, was the work of a bungling amateur. Which could describe anyone in the Arbuthnot ménage—and why not? Outwardly respectable, upper-middle-class people might be moderately expert at tennis, bridge or golf, but breaking and entering was not usually numbered among their accomplishments. They were bound to fumble a bit on the first attempt.

The first? Did she really think there would be others? She considered the question coldly for a moment and decided that the answer was: probably. They might not have been sure there was a cat on the premises prior to that silent telephone call, but someone was certain now.

"You've blown the gaff," she told Sassy resignedly. "Now we're for it."

Sassy looked at her blankly, then strolled away to resume her vigil by the door. It was nothing to do with her; she was as good as out of here. Just as soon as Mummy arrived.

"It's all right for some," Annabel muttered. "But we're stuck here and you've given the game away." She looked around, with some vague idea of barricading the door with the sofa overnight, in case the would-be intruder tried again. It was obviously impossible to rely on the locked front entrance—there might as well be a "Welcome Burglars" mat displayed. She had seen for herself just how easy it was to gain access thanks to an obliging resident.

For a female, that is. A toss of the hair, a roll of the eyes, a charming pout—and the unregenerate sexists in this building would roll out the red carpet. The finger of suspicion swung towards Kelda again.

On the other hand, a man brandishing some sort of spurious identification could pass himself off as a plumber or electrician answering an emergency call. He might even be carrying a case containing the tools he had used to try to break open the door. A case in which a cat could be concealed and carried away.

It was growing darker outside, rain clouds had been gathering slowly and determinedly, forging themselves into an overall deep grey ceiling which was about to open up and release the deluge. Even as she noticed this, the first heavy drops splattered against the windows.

Did that mean she ought to put on the lights and draw the curtains? Rather, first the curtains, then the lights, so that no one could look up and see that she was home—she had been caught that way last night.

Perhaps not just yet. There was movement in the street below. A Range Rover had turned into the street and was driving along slowly, as though the driver were trying to read the block numbers through the rain.

Across the room, Sassy suddenly turned her head and looked towards the window.

There was one parking place on the other side of the street and the Range Rover pulled into it. Sassy left her post and came to join Annabel at the window, chattering excitedly.

"Yes, I think so, too," Annabel said. Together, they watched as the Range Rover door swung open and a tall thin woman hopped out, holding what looked like a collapsible cat carrier over her head to protect her hairdo from the worst of the downpour. She darted across the street and up the steps to the apartment block. A few seconds later, the doorbell rang.

"Mmrrraaah!" Sassy streaked across the room, shrieking to Annabel to follow and be quick about it.

The buzzer sounded again and, with only a perfunctory glance at the tiny TV screen, Annabel pushed the lock release, then watched the woman dive through the door and disappear into the hall.

Sassy scurried back and forth between Annabel and the door, uttering urgent little cries. The other two cats had moved some distance away, Annabel noticed, and were observing the scene from the shelter of the kitchen doorway.

When the inner doorbell sounded, Sassy leaped forward, nearly tripping Annabel, and yowling excitedly.

"Sassy! Sassy, darling!" No less excited cries came from the other side of the door. "Here I am! Mummy's here!"

Annabel managed to wrench the door open and stood back. Sassy hurled herself forward, leaped for the hem of the tweed skirt and clawed herself upwards and into the waiting arms. The nylon cat carrier hit the floor as Sassy filled the woman's arms. The woman and cat purred and cooed at each other, lost in a world of their own.

Annabel cleared her throat, there seemed to be a lump in it. She closed the door behind them and bent to pick up the carrier, which shook itself out into a flat-bottomed bag which might have been used for sports equipment were it not for the fine mesh at one end. A cat could settle down and watch the world go by when she was being carried along in this. Annabel nodded approval.

"I can't thank you enough!" The woman remembered her suddenly and swung to face her, still clutching Sassy. "I was so worried. I was frantic. I thought I'd lost her. I'm so grateful. Are you sure I can't give you the reward?"

"I wouldn't dream of taking anything," Annabel said firmly. "Just seeing Sassy back in her rightful place is enough for me."

"Oh—" The woman looked beyond Annabel and her smile grew even wider. "You have cats of your own. Of course, you understand."

"They're not exactly—" Annabel began, then let it go. Sally and Salvatore were not to be explained. "Can I offer you a drink?" she suggested instead.

"You are kind, but I'm driving and I really must get back, if you don't mind. My husband has been so worried, too. He can't wait to see Sassy again."

"Quite all right," Annabel assured her. "Here, let me help—" Sassy did not want to abandon those loving arms long enough to allow them to put her into her carrying case. Annabel unzipped the case and held it open while the woman lowered Sassy into it. There was a slight tussle as Sassy protested.

"Now be a good girl, Sassy," the woman told her, "and we'll soon be home."

Annabel pushed Sassy's head down firmly and zipped the bag shut. Sassy immediately began complaining loudly.

"Thank you again," the woman said. "If there's ever anything I can do for you, just call me."

"That's all right," Annabel said. "It was my pleasure." She did not add that a great part of the pleasure was seeing the last of Sassy and knowing that there was going to be some peace and quiet around here now. She suspected she was not the only one to feel that way; a quiet sense of satisfaction seemed to radiate from the other cats as they watched Sassy depart.

Annabel went over to the window to pull the curtains. The rain had settled down into a tropical downpour and she watched the woman run across the street and leap into her Range Rover. Even from this distance, she could hear Sassy's voice, and even after the door had slammed.

The motor roared to life, the headlights flashed on and the Range Rover moved forward, swung out, seemed to dither a moment, then made a U-turn and drove off.

Seconds later, another car, small, dark and inconspicuous, also started up, moved forward and duplicated the U-turn. This one did not put its headlights on. It slid silently in the wake of the Range Rover until the big vehicle turned into the main road. Then the smaller headlights lit up and the car followed the Range Rover out into the mainstream traffic.

"Well . . . what do you think of that?" Annabel drew the curtains, no longer sure that it was necessary.

The cats looked up at her, their bright eyes twinkled affection, but they kept their opinions to themselves and moved off towards the kitchen.

Annabel knew what she thought: the driver of the second car had been her intruder, lurking in his vehicle, hoping she would leave the flat again and give him another chance to break in and begin his interrupted search.

It was someone after Sally, of course. Someone who suspected Annabel of harbouring her. Someone who, hearing Sassy's loud cries as she was carried across the road and unable to differentiate one cat from another, now believed that Annabel had passed Sally on to a friend to hide. That was why he had abandoned his surveillance. He was going to follow that poor woman home and try to get the cat away from her.

And that would be a fight worth seeing. No one was ever going to part Sassy from her mistress again. Not only that, but Annabel had the strong impression that the woman lived in the sort of establishment that came equipped with high-tech security equipment and probably guards.

Just the same . . .

She still had the telephone number. Should she ring the woman and warn her? Or was she overreacting? It was quite possible that the dark car belonged to some innocent party, who was just happening to pull out at the same time and copied the U-turn because it looked like a good idea. Annabel told herself sternly that she had no real reason to think that the car intended to follow the Range Rover—nor, given the level of competence displayed thus far, to think that it had any hope of succeeding.

Annabel adjusted the drapes so that no chink of light would show, and turned away from the windows, becoming aware of the cats watching her hopefully from the kitchen doorway.

"You're hungry, I suppose," she said, as they fell in on either side of her and escorted her to the fridge.

"I was going to buy some tins of cat food for you, but I was being watched, so it wasn't safe." She opened the freezer section and rummaged inside. "You'll just have to take pot luck."

Frozen cauliflower and broccoli florets, peas, corn, a half leg of lamb—it would take for ever to defrost. However, she transferred it to the fridge, it would do for tomorrow's dinner, since she was planning to hole up here for the rest of the weekend.

With a guilty pang, Annabel realized how thoroughly she was depleting Dinah's supplies; she'd have to replace them before she left. That was why she was trying to go lightly on those delicious one-serving homemade meals the housekeeper had left prepared for Dinah. The odd chop, steak or roast could be easily replaced; she didn't fancy the thought of doing a lot of heavy shopping to restock the freezer. Although that venison stew looked awfully tempting—and the cats would probably like it, too.

"Ah, this should do!" She straightened triumphantly, clutching a large packet of prawns. "I'll try to pick up some cat food for you later—" She broke off, not just at the sudden realization that there wasn't. going to be much of a later, not after Monday, but also because the cats had looked at each other and were now regarding her with what she could swear was amusement.

For a moment, she put herself in the cats' position and recognized the joke: she was apologizing for serving them large luscious prawns instead of tinned food.

Salvatore ambled over and head-butted her ankles fondly. He loved a woman with a sense of humour.

16

Sunday—and she'd promised herself that it would be a peaceful day of rest. After opening the door to take in the newspaper, Annabel pulled up the drawbridge mentally, safe in her borrowed castle for the day. She stretched out on the sofa, dissecting the paper, discarding the Appointments, Sports and Children's sections, and settled down for a good read. The cats were having a game with their catnip mouse, the aroma of roasting lamb was beginning to permeate the air and, outside, it was still raining, the sort of steady persistent downpour that added to the contentment of those who were comfortably inside their dwellings with no need to venture out that day.

A sudden gust of wind slammed rain against the windows. The cats stopped playing and went to investigate. Annabel was suddenly aware of just how precarious her safe haven might be. If anyone were to look up, the cats could be seen from the street below.

"No!" Annabel fought free of the theatre section and dashed over to pull them back out of sight. "Don't do that!" She peered out through the curtain of rain, which was obviously having a dampening effect on anyone who might have considered lurking below. The street was deserted.

"Why don't you take a catnap?" She carried the cats over to the sofa and deposited them on it, then stretched out again herself. Sally curled up where she had landed and obligingly went to sleep. Salvatore inched upwards until his head rested on her shoulder and closed his eyes in bliss. Annabel absently nuzzled the top of his head with her chin and went back to the theatre pages, wondering if the new play previewing this week was going to be worth the effort of getting to an early performance. The cast was good, but the playwright was unknown.

The sudden buzz of the downstairs doorbell startled them all.

"Now what?" Disentangling herself from cats and broadsheets, Annabel stumbled over to check the entryview screen. No one she knew, but the young woman's face was partially obscured by the oversized flower arrangement she carried.

A quick check out of the window revealed a genuine florist's van outside the building and Annabel judged it safe to push the lock release. A few moments later, she was opening the door to receive the arrangement, which was even more enormous than it had looked on the screen.

"Have a nice day!" the messenger burbled and dashed away—so quickly that, for a paranoid instant, Annabel wondered whether the flowers were booby-trapped.

Gingerly, Annabel managed to get it over to the

table, it was almost too awkward to carry and the fact that the cats had come to investigate and were underfoot didn't help. She set it down and stepped back to survey it, finally sighting the small white square nearly concealed in the lower foliage.

> ## "A MILLION THANKS
> ## FROM
> ## SASSY AND HER MUMMY"

Turning the card over, Annabel whistled with surprise at the name engraved on the other side. The lady could, indeed, afford to give a million of anything; between them, she and her husband owned a large chunk of Canada.

An additional scribbled message assured Annabel, once she had deciphered it, that Sassy's mummy was eternally in her debt and could be called on at any time.

"That may be useful," Annabel murmured thoughtfully.

Salvatore leaped up to investigate and disagreed; it wasn't edible. Sally joined him and sniffed delicately at a few blooms so exotic that Annabel could not even put a name to them, but seemed to approve. They circled the arrangement, then Salvatore decided to give one of the flowers a second chance. He nipped off a petal, chewed thoughtfully, then spat it out in disgust. He had been right the first time. He strolled to the edge of the table and leaped over to the bookcase, settling full length along one of the not-too-crowded shelves, his tail dangling off the edge.

Sally took another turn around the flower arrangement, still sniffing, until she decided which bloom she favoured and curled up beneath it with a yawn. It was nap time again.

Annabel yawned in sympathy and decided that the cats had the right idea. A nice little snooze was just the thing on a day like this. The sofa was calling . . .

First, though, she went over to check on Salvatore; his position on that shelf looked rather perilous. If he rolled over, he would be on the floor. Perhaps she ought to move some of those books, so that he had the shelf to himself.

"Sorry to disturb you," she said, reaching over him to remove some books, "but you'll be more comfortable when I finish."

Salvatore lifted his head and opened one eye halfway, giving her the benefit of his affable leer. She could do anything she wanted. He closed his eye again and allowed her to slide him to the back of the shelf, purring his thanks.

Annabel deposited her armload of books on the side of the table Sally wasn't using. They were a mixed bag of bestsellers out of the mists of time. Probably Dinah's husband had been the book buyer in the family, biography and adventure figured largely.

One of the books caught her attention, triggering a nagging irritation that she had ignored in the press of more urgent events. She removed the book from the pile and brought it over to the sofa, where she stretched out and looked at it with grim satisfaction. She knew just who this book ought to go to—one could only hope that he would get the message.

Reach For the Sky was the biography of Douglas Bader, the pilot who had lost both legs, got himself fitted with artificial ones and learned to walk again. No moping around in a wheelchair feeling sorry for himself for *him*. He had even taken to the sky again, fought in the Battle of Britain, been shot down over occupied France, and escaped from his blazing aircraft, ironically enough, by leaving his hopelessly trapped artificial leg behind. Not surprisingly, he was captured by the Germans, who, in one of the more honourable incidents in that deadly conflict, communicated with London, where arrangements were made for a replacement leg to be parachuted down for him.

Yes, indeed, it might be very salutary for Mark to read this story. The young so often assumed that no one else had ever had the troubles they faced, that they were alone in an uncharted wilderness without a compass.

Annabel hadn't realized she had fallen into a doze until she was rudely awakened. *Damn!* She should have unplugged the telephone before lying down. She contemplated not answering, instinctively feeling that this disturbance of her peace on a quiet Sunday afternoon boded no good. She had no desire for another session with the heavy breather. On the other hand, if she did not answer, he might appear in person, thinking the flat was empty. The thought brought her to her feet.

"Annabel!" The long wait for an answer had not improved Xanthippe's temper. "What are you doing there?"

"Having a quiet Sunday. At least, I was."

"Wasting your time, you mean," Xanthippe corrected. "Why aren't you with the Arbuthnots?"

"Why should I be?"

"Because they're cremating Arthur Arbuthnot."

"On a Sunday?" Annabel was startled. "Isn't that unusual?"

"The rich are different, Annabel. You should know that by now. Hopewell run their own crematorium in tandem with their medical establishments. And if the Arbuthnots want to order a cremation on a Sunday, none of the hirelings is going to quibble about the day of the week. They know which side their bread is buttered on."

Yes, hirelings would—and not only those on the lower levels. There had been rumours that certain doctors at Hopewell clinics had been struck off the register of various countries because of an excessively casual attitude towards reporting such things as gunshot wounds, communicable disease and, of course, knife wounds.

"So the cremation is just a family affair." Annabel pulled her attention back to the immediate situation. "Very private. Why am I not surprised?" She should have guessed this would happen. Annabel remembered now the strained look on Tara's face when she mentioned that today was going to be a "Hell Day." This must have been what she was referring to.

"Where are your doorsteppers?" Annabel sailed into the offensive. "Cindy and Sid. Aren't they there?"

"Too identifiable," Xanthippe said. "If they blow

their cover showing up there, they won't be able to work at the flat again."

"You think they work, do you?" But the riposte was automatic, the full implications of the situation were becoming apparent: the family were disposing of the evidence. A cremated body could not be exhumed and examined at a later date when enough suspicion of foul play had surfaced to call for police intervention.

"We're losing the story!" Xanthippe snapped. "What are we going to do?"

"Difficult, isn't it?" Annabel sympathized. "But I don't see what could be done, even if we attended the service. It isn't like a wedding, you know. The minister isn't going to say, 'If anyone can show just cause why this body should not be cremated, let him speak now or for ever hold his peace,' or whatever."

"Tchah!" Xanthippe made an explosive little sound of annoyance. "I wish you'd try to be serious, Annabel."

"Oh, I'm very serious," Annabel assured her, and she was. Someone was going to get away with murder. The murder of a man she had known and liked. Oh, undoubtedly he had been difficult and overbearing in his relations with other people, but he had been all right with her. Perhaps, if she had known him longer, she might have discovered his harsher side, but it seemed unfair and unjust that someone should be able to kill him and then destroy the body so that he escaped all consequences.

On the other hand, how much could the body have betrayed? The private medical institution had obviously been able to keep Arthur Arbuthnot in some semblance of life for several days on their high-tech machines. Would that have been long enough for any knife wound in his back to have healed naturally? It was possible, Annabel supposed, which would make it even more unlikely that the police would be able—or willing—to do anything.

Of course, there was still Dora Stringer's body. No one was going to worry too much about her. But a push wouldn't show up in any autopsy—not even a sudden and violent push—unless she had bruised easily. And even then, a bruise or two would prove nothing—

"Annabel? Are you still there?"

"Just thinking," Annabel said.

"And—?"

"And nothing, I'm afraid. Nothing we can prove, nothing we can do, nothing . . ." Annabel glanced at her watch: four-thirty-five. "In any case, the cremation must be over by now. You've left it a bit late to call, haven't you?"

"I've just got in and found the information on my answering machine. I couldn't call earlier. I'd hoped you would have been there."

"Who left the message?"

"I think it was Cindy." Xanthippe hesitated. "The voice was rather blurred, not a good line, probably on her mobile, but it was a woman's voice. It must have been Cindy."

So much for the other source of information about the Arbuthnots Xanthippe had claimed she had. Annabel had suspected she had been bluffing, now she was sure. There was no other mole in the Arbuthnot ménage—at least, not one that Xanthippe was aware of.

"Annabel? Don't do that!"

"Do what?"

"Go off into those long silences when I'm trying to hold a conversation with you."

"Sorry." Now that she knew it bothered Xanthippe, Annabel made a mental note to do it more often. "Just thinking."

"Thinking what? What are you going to do?"

"I'm going to have a peaceful Sunday—what's left of it. Goodbye." Annabel replaced the receiver and strode over to pull the plug out of its socket. There! She should have disconnected the phone much earlier.

That done, she stood irresolute for a moment, looking around the room as though she might find some answer. The cats were awake and alert again. They looked at her with interest.

"Oh, Sally," she sighed. "If only you could tell me what you know." Sally blinked back at her, inscrutable.

"Oh, well," Annabel said. "What do we do now?"

The cats were in no doubt. As one, they leaped to the floor from their respective perches and marched kitchenwards.

We eat.

17

Kelda and Mark were deep in conversation behind the reception desk when Annabel arrived in the morning. Close together, heads bent, they looked almost furtive. Their conversation was too low to be overheard. Pity, it might have been interesting.

"I'm glad you're both here." Annabel noted the way they jumped apart guiltily. They had obviously been too absorbed in each other to notice her approach.

"I have something"—Annabel reached into her basket and brought out the Bader biography—"that I think you both ought to read." She set it down in front of Mark emphatically. "Especially you," she told him.

Kelda started back with a strange mewling cry. Mark glared at both of them and cleared his throat loudly. It seemed the Bader story was not unknown to them; perhaps it had already been the subject of some discussion.

"What do you think you're playing at?" Mark demanded. His face was turning quite red.

"Mark, please—" It was a strangulated cadence

that did not sound quite right. Kelda tried again. "Please. Annabel is only trying to be helpful."

"She's not helping *me*. Go on, clear off!" He waved Annabel away. "Go upstairs and meddle with *them*. Leave me alone!"

"Perhaps you'd better go up," Kelda said pleadingly. "I'll follow along shortly. I just want to have another word with Mark." She put a tentative hand on his shoulder, as though to calm him.

"Don't be too long," Annabel said, just to exert some authority. She was pleased to notice that they had not returned the book.

Upstairs, there was muted chaos. Cindy and Sid were trying to look fully occupied while lurking in the doorway of the drawing room.

"Aren't you wanted anywhere else?" Annabel demanded crossly. "Or are you planning to take up residence here?"

"Look who got up on the wrong side of bed this morning," Sid jeered.

"What a surprise," Cindy said. "The right side is probably pushed up against the wall."

Take it whence it comes, Annabel. She contented herself with giving them a look which should have struck them to the floor, but it merely glanced off their rhinoceros hides, and turned away. There was too much at stake today to worry about unruly minions. Except, they weren't really minions—they were paparazzi and dangerous.

"Anyway, we *are* working." Cindy brandished a dripping paintbrush defensively.

"Mmmm," was as much as Annabel would commit herself to. She didn't know all that much about it, but she had the vague impression that one didn't start painting the skirting boards before one had done anything to the walls.

"Did Kelda tell you to do that?" she asked.

"She's been too busy to talk to us today," Sid said. "Makes you wonder what she's up to, doesn't it?"

Actually, it did, but Annabel wasn't going to admit that. Fortunately, no one in England was ever surprised at discovering that their workmen were completely incompetent and had done a bodged job. Dismayed, yes; surprised, no. Whoever inherited the place, via the lovely Sally, would just have to sort it out later.

Certainly, no one around here was going to worry about anything so mundane at the moment.

"Since you've started on your natural habitat—the woodwork—you might as well do the door now," Annabel said, closing it firmly behind her. With any luck, they might paint the door shut and be stuck inside. Reluctantly, Annabel banished a tantalizing vision of two skeletons being discovered several decades from now and pulled her attention back to business.

This was a day to lurk in whatever shadows she could find, as close to the study as possible. Annabel carried her basket down to the very end of the corridor, removed the tape measure and notebook, knelt and hunched over, trying to make herself as small and inconspicuous as possible. If she remained below eye level, obviously absorbed in her work, it was just possible that everyone would be too intent on their own concerns to notice her.

She hadn't long to wait. She felt the vibration of their tread shudder along the floorboards before she looked up and saw them. She hadn't expected Mr. Pennyman to bring a colleague with him, but it made sense, given the circumstances. Safety in numbers, and all that. Poor Mr. Pennyman had obviously learned his lesson in that first session of dealing with Arthur Arbuthnot's heirs en masse. He couldn't be blamed for wanting someone along who would be on his side.

But it upset the vague plan Annabel had made. She had wanted to intercept Mr. Pennyman for a private conversation, before he dealt with the family. There was no chance of that now.

Also, Luther was there in the lead, opening the study door and ushering them inside. "You're a bit early," he said. "I'll tell the others you've arrived." He closed the door firmly and went back down the hallway, so deep in some thoughts of his own that he hadn't even noticed Annabel.

The others appeared almost immediately, but stood huddled in a defensive group at the far end of the hallway, seemingly bracing themselves before advancing on the study.

Uncle Wystan was in the middle of the group, carrying what looked like a large jewel box. Zenia and Tara suddenly flourished handkerchiefs.

Annabel's nose wrinkled as a sudden whiff of onions eddied towards her. Odd, the kitchen was in the basement and no cooking smells had ever reached the upper floors before.

" 'Forward the Light Brigade'," Cousin Neville gave the order.

Tara dabbed gently at her nose and gave a loud sniff.

"No need to overdo it, old girl," Wystan said.

With measured tread, Uncle Wystan advanced solemnly, the others falling into step behind him. Luther brought up the rear, stepping forward at the last moment to throw open the study door, still with that look of abstraction. They all marched into the study.

Annabel hurled herself forward and managed to shove a corner of her notebook into the opening in time to prevent the door closing completely. The smell of onions was stronger than ever.

Annabel slid the notebook out of the aperture and pushed the door open a little wider. Now she had a partial view of what was going on, as well as being able to hear everything.

"I am the bearer of sad tidings," she heard Wystan announce, just before he stepped into view to set the jewel box down on the library table in front of Mr. Pennyman.

"Poor, dear little Sally—" Tara murmured, breaking off with a tearful sniff.

"These things happen," Neville said.

"Sad, very sad." Wystan swung the lid of the box up and they all crowded round to look down at its contents.

"Most unfortunate," Mr. Pennyman agreed. "How did it happen?"

"She got out when we weren't watching," Tara said. "We were shattered when we discovered it. We looked everywhere for her, but we couldn't find her. Then . . . then . . ." She dabbed at her eyes, at her nose, with her handkerchief.

Mr. Pennyman coughed and stepped back slightly as a wave of onion scent threatened to overwhelm him. Tara was overdoing it, indeed. Annabel could feel her own eyes smarting. At this rate, the whole group would soon be racked by onion-induced grief.

"In the street." Neville put his arm around Tara comfortingly. "By the kerb, actually. Poor little thing must have been hit by a car. Accident. These things happen."

"So you said." Mr. Pennyman gave him a shrewd look. "Pity you couldn't have found her sooner. While she was still alive."

"We can only be thankful that poor Arthur isn't here to see this day," Wystan said. "It would have killed him."

"If Arthur had been alive, it wouldn't have happened," Zenia pointed out. "It was his death, and then Dora's, that upset the household routine so much. People coming and going, leaving doors open. The police and, of course," she added venomously, "the decorators."

"It really wasn't our fault," Tara protested tearfully. "We tried our best to find her. We looked everywhere."

Mr. Pennyman's companion had moved forward and was frowning down into the jewel casket. He bent over and reached inside, seemingly prodding the body, then straightened up.

"You can keep looking," he said. "This isn't Sally."

Some instinct made Annabel step aside a split second before the door swung wide and Luther slipped out of the study. He took off down the corridor at a jogging pace, looking neither left nor right, an aura of determination surrounding him.

"What?"

"Of course it is!"

"How do you know?"

"Forgive me," Mr. Pennyman said. "I should have introduced my, er, associate, earlier. This is Mr. Tilbury, Arthur's—and Sally's—veterinarian."

The casket lid fell with a snap that reverberated through the sudden silence.

"Oh, thank heavens!" Tara recovered first. She tucked her handkerchief into her handbag with an air of relief. "Then perhaps we can still find Sally alive."

"We can hope," Wystan said unconvincingly. "While there's life, there's . . . that is, if she *is* still alive."

Zenia's explosive snort had nothing to do with the onion slices in her own handkerchief. "I just hope you know what you're doing!" She glared impartially at her husband, at Mr. Pennyman and at the veterinarian; it wasn't clear which one she was addressing.

Mr. Pennyman cleared his throat, a vague noncommittal sound, playing for time, promising nothing. Mr. Tilbury looked at him, then at the others, and waited for further elucidation.

"Annabel—get out of the way!" The command

came from behind her, and Annabel whirled around to find Kelda and Mark poised to roll into the study as soon as she stopped blocking their way. Mark had a small carrying case in his lap.

"Don't say anything," Kelda warned. "Keep out of this! Just let us pass."

Annabel could feel her eyes widening as she stared at the wire-mesh end of the case, there was soft furry movement behind it. She stepped aside automatically, allowing Mark to sweep into the study, Kelda immediately behind him.

"Ah!" Mr. Pennyman looked at them without surprise. "And what have we here?"

"Sally," Kelda said, when Mark did not respond quickly enough. "It's Sally. She always liked Mark and she came to him for protection after Mr. Arbuthnot died."

"Indeed?" Mr. Pennyman became blander than ever. "Well, suppose you let us have a look at the little lady?"

"Right." Mark fumbled with the latch and finally opened the mesh door. When nothing happened, he reached inside and seemed to engage in a slight struggle. A severe bout of foul language issued from the case and Mark dragged a protesting tabby from its depths. Once out, she shook her bristling fur back into a semblance of smoothness and looked around warily.

"Oh, I say!" Wystan choked. "That's a bit much! Abducting our cat like that."

The cat wasn't a bad match. If Annabel had not been in close proximity to the real Sally for the past few days, even she might have been fooled. People to whom the cat had been nothing more than an annoy-ance underfoot were more easily duped. They re-garded the cat—and then Mark—with varying degrees of hostility.

"Sally, darling—" Tara started forward and the cat shrank back.

"That isn't Sally." Zenia sounded as though she spoke more from hope than from conviction.

"No." Mr. Tilbury stared at the one white paw which did not match up with Sally's markings. "I don't believe it is."

"A good try," Neville sneered at Mark. "But not quite good enough. Anyone in the family would know that isn't Sally."

"How could it be—?" Luther stood in the doorway, cradling a cat in his arms. "When I have Sally right here?"

The world was full of tabby cats! Annabel reeled as she realized what this did to her plans. How could she show up with Sally now? No one would ever be-lieve her. They'd think she was just another chancer. She'd be laughed out of court, out of town. And poor little Sally would never come into her rightful inher-itance.

"You slimy, double-crossing creep!" Neville snarled at Luther.

"Fascinating!" Mr. Pennyman had steepled his fin-gers and was gazing over them, as though looking down on an alien world of Lilliputians. "How Arthur would have enjoyed this."

This cat was a winsome little creature and, unlike the other, obviously happy and comfortable in familiar arms. Also, it was a perfect double for Sally. Annabel wondered how long it had taken Luther to find her—and how long he had had her.

"I always took care of Sally when Mr. Arbuthnot was busy," Luther said. "Didn't I, sweetheart?" He lowered his head to hers and she rubbed against his chin with a fond purr. Yes, she knew him well, loved and trusted him. In fact, she was his cat; it was doubtful that she had ever encountered Arthur Arbuthnot in all of her short life.

"These others—" Luther gave the family a scornful, dismissive glance. "They never cared for Sally at all. Not until they thought they could use her."

How long had Luther been plotting this? And which had come first, the cat or the plot? It was obvious that he had known the major dispensations in Arthur Arbuthnot's will. Had he deliberately gone looking for a cat that would be Sally's double, or had he found the cat first and then realized he could replace Sally? Was that why he had been searching so desperately among the dustbins? If he had found Sally then, would he have done away with her and replaced her with this cat so obviously devoted to him and who would run to him, given a choice of owners?

But . . . however clever the scheme, it could only take effect after Arthur Arbuthnot was dead and, in the normal course of events, Arthur could have lived another couple of decades. Moreover, although the stakes were high, the outcome couldn't be guaranteed. Would Luther really have murdered Arthur Arbuthnot on the off-chance that he could swap cats and thus control the financial empire? Did he imagine that the family would stand by quietly and allow him to get away with it?

"That cat is ours!" Zenia advanced on Luther with deadly purpose. "Hand it over!"

The cat shrank back against Luther for protection as Zenia reached out to snatch at it. Luther took a step backwards and half turned, presenting his shoulder to Zenia and sheltering the cat.

"That's right!" Neville moved forward on Luther's other side. "Give it here!"

"You really had better, old boy," Wystan weighed in. "You know you can't possibly get away with keeping it."

"Sally has the right to choose which of us is to be her guardian." Luther faced them all with steely determination. "It says so in Arthur's will."

By this time, Annabel had been drawn forward irresistibly and was now standing inside the study with her back against the wall. Only the faintest flicker of Mr. Pennyman's eyelids showed that he had noticed her. No one else had.

"He meant one of us—not you!" Zenia was incandescent with fury.

"Possession"—Luther smirked—"is—"

"We'll see about that!" Neville snarled.

"Tilbury," Mr. Pennyman interrupted with quiet authority, "what's your opinion?"

"Closer, much closer. In fact, possible." Mr. Tilbury went up to Luther. "Let's have a better look at you . . . Sally."

The little cat cocked her head and watched him approach. No doubt about it, she was a man's cat and her name was definitely Sally. But then, it would be, wouldn't it?

Luther held on to his cat protectively, making soothing little noises deep in his throat as the veterinarian stroked and prodded. Luther was human, after all, Annabel decided. Wherever he had found the cat and whatever plans he had made for her, the bonding had worked both ways, he really cared about her.

"Hmmm . . ." Tilbury was probing between her shoulder blades with a thoughtful expression. "Let me just . . ." He stooped and opened a small satchel, bringing out something that looked to Annabel like one of the early hand-held hair dryers.

"It's all right, Sally," Luther assured his little pet. "It won't hurt you." He glared at Tilbury sharply. "Will it?"

"Not a bit." Tilbury moved his gadget up and down the length of the cat's spine, from between the ears to the tail, several times, then switched it off and looked over to Mr. Pennyman.

"No." He scratched Sally's ears. "You're a beautiful, healthy little cat with a sweet nature—"

Luther snuggled the cat a little closer, preening.

"But you're not the right Sally," Tilbury concluded.

"I always knew you were a crook!" Neville snarled at Luther. "I'll see to it you never get another job in this town!"

"Oh?" Luther laughed out loud. "Who do you imagine would listen to you? I've already had several approaches, not to mention offers from New York, Frankfurt, Paris and Vancouver." He laughed again. "And none of them ever heard of *you*."

"We'll see about that!" Even to himself, the reply must have sounded pretty feeble for, still fuming, Neville looked around for someone else to vent his rage on.

"And you—" His gaze fell upon Annabel. "You're fired! I'll see to it that you never decorate another flat for the rest of your life!"

"That's all right with me." Annabel smiled sweetly. Neville would never know how little terror his threat held. "I was thinking of retiring, anyway."

"As you can afford to," Zenia said coldly, "considering the amount of non-declarable cash you've made away with."

"Now wait a minute!" Annabel was not prepared to let that pass. There had been too many nasty suggestions about the size of her remuneration. "Mr. Arbuthnot only paid me a basic retainer which isn't going to cover—"

"I'm not referring to that!" Zenia cut her off. "I'm talking about all the cash you helped yourself to from the safe in his study!"

Mr. Pennyman cleared his throat, an unassuming sound that, this time, somehow spoke volumes about false accusations, slander, defamation of character and long expensive lawsuits.

Zenia closed her mouth abruptly.

That safe! By a great effort of will, Annabel kept herself from glancing in its direction—which would surely be taken as an indication of guilt. Suddenly all the snide insinuations began to make sense. The Broomstick had been the first, with her flat statement that Annabel had been paid enough to hang the walls with ermine. Was that what she had believed when she had checked the safe and found it empty? That Annabel had been given—or had taken—the contents of the safe?

But perhaps the Broomstick had found out, or suspected, differently later. That could be why she had died. One forgot, blinded by the vast total of the entire estate, that there were those to whom the hundreds of thousands worth of domestic and foreign currency stashed away in the safe was an amount worth absconding with.

Annabel opened her mouth to point this out, but was forestalled.

"I don't see the difference." Kelda looked from Luther's Sally to her own nominee and voiced her grievance. "They both look alike to me. I'm sure *we've* got the right Sally. You didn't even try her out with that thing you've got."

"Oh, very well." Tilbury approached the cat in Mark's lap. Unlike Luther's Sally, this was not a happy cat. It bristled its fur as Tilbury drew closer and hissed warningly.

"All right, all right, this won't take a minute." Tilbury ran the scanner over it and frowned in surprise. "Well!"

Annabel edged closer. She could see movement on the tiny visual display screen of his instrument.

"Not Sally," he said, "and definitely not Arthur Arbuthnot's, but, as soon as I can call her up on my central registry, I can tell you who she does belong to."

"I told you it wouldn't work!" Mark snapped at

Kelda. "This was all a waste of time and effort. All those stupid excuses you gave for borrowing—"

"Or perhaps you already know the owner," Tilbury said.

"She's a friend of mine." Kelda admitted defeat. "The cat looked so much like Sally . . . I told her I wanted to use it as a model for a different kind of picture than the ones I usually paint."

"But what would you have done if the cat had been accepted as Sally?" Annabel was too curious to keep quiet. "You wouldn't have been able to give it back then."

"We'd have come to some arrangement." Kelda shrugged. "I would never have bothered if I'd known she'd had the damned thing booby-trapped."

"Microchipped, actually," Tilbury corrected. "More and more owners are having it done these days, thank goodness. Then if the pet gets lost and separated from its collar, it can still be identified and returned to its owner."

"And Arthur Arbuthnot had Sally microchipped?" Annabel felt giddy with relief. The real Sally could prove who she was.

"Arthur insisted on it, before I even had a chance to suggest it to him. He didn't want to risk losing Sally; he said she was too good a cat to go back to that alley."

"In that case"—Annabel turned to Mr. Pennyman—"I have something to tell you."

"Ah, yes," he said without surprise. "I rather thought you might have."

18

There were too many people here, Annabel thought resentfully. And most of them self-invited.

Bristling with mistrust, Zenia and Neville had stalked in and glared around the Knightsbridge drawing room. Wystan trailed unhappily in their wake. A strangely subdued Tara sank into the corner of the sofa she had occupied on her last visit and seemed to detach herself from the proceedings.

Kelda stood protectively behind Mark's wheelchair, while Luther lounged against a wall and watched. Annabel still wasn't sure what they were doing here—or what they had done with their respective Sally candidates.

Messrs Pennyman and Tilbury looked at Annabel expectantly.

Annabel looked back at them, momentarily blank. Although she would have liked a drink herself, she was damned if she was going to offer one to any of these interlopers. They had pushed their way in here and she was not going to appear to ratify their presence. They were pests, not guests.

"Let's get this over with," Zenia said brusquely. "Where is this cat you claim is Sally?"

The entrance doorbell buzzed . . . and buzzed . . . and buzzed . . . urgently and persistently. It was not going to stop until someone was admitted. With a sinking heart and a gloomy conviction that she knew who it was, Annabel crossed to the window and looked down.

"There she is!" Cindy spotted her. "Let us in! Annabel! Let us in!" The doorbell settled down to a long steady buzz.

"What are they doing here?" Zenia demanded. "They haven't done something dreadful to the flat, have they? You should never have left them there unsupervised."

"Ignore them," Annabel advised, raising her voice above the buzzing. Doorsteppers, Xanthippe had called them—and the doorstep was where they belonged.

"They won't go away," Kelda warned.

"Then you go down and deal with them!" Annabel lost what little patience remained. "And stop them ringing that doorbell!"

"I think they've stuck a pin in it. It will fall out eventually." It was clear that Kelda did not intend to miss anything that was happening up here.

"That's not Sally!" Wystan said suddenly, as Salvatore sauntered into the room to see what all the commotion was about. "It's the other one, the chap I found. Here, old chap, come and say hello." He snapped his fingers encouragingly.

Salvatore lifted his head and curled his lip, giving

Wystan a *Have-we-met?* look, and detoured around him to sniff at Mark's wheelchair.

"Silly woman, made off with the wrong cat," Wystan chortled, not noticing that he'd been cut dead.

"So did you," his wife reminded him. Something in her tone implied a deeper meaning.

"If we might proceed ... ?" Mr. Pennyman frowned at his watch. "I take it there is another cat? A female one?"

"Sally ... ?" the veterinarian called softly. "Sally ... you can come out now. We're all friends here."

Sally knew better. Or possibly she hadn't heard his voice above the maddeningly insistent buzzing.

"Can't anyone stop that racket?" Zenia complained.

"Oh, right!" Abruptly galvanized into action, Wystan went over to the entryscreen and yanked with suppressed violence at the wires. The entryscreen went blank, but the buzzing stopped.

Silence ... beautiful silence. Everyone seemed to breathe more easily.

"That's better, eh?" Wystan blinked diffidently at them. "Sorry about any damage," he apologized to Annabel. "We'll pay for it of—"

"Wystan!" Zenia cut across his apology. "She can pay for it herself. She's made off with enough to—"

Mr. Pennyman cleared his throat again.

Something hit the windows sharply. Cindy and Sid must have found some pebbles, or perhaps they were throwing coins. It was to be hoped the windows did not break. Broken wires were bad enough.

"Sally ... ? Sally ... ?" Tilbury was not to be distracted by minor problems. "Sally ... ?"

Annabel was the first to spot the tiny nose poking around the corner. Salvatore saw it next and went over to give it an encouraging lick and to usher his friend into the room.

Just inside the doorway, Sally stopped and looked around. Her ears flattened and her fur began to rise, her tail brushed out.

"All right, Sally, it's all right, girl," the vet soothed. "Come over here and let's look at you."

Sally had to pass Tara, Zenia, Wystan and Neville to reach him. Her fur rose higher at every step until she looked like a fur football.

"That isn't Sally, either," Wystan said. "It's one of those fancy breeds, Persian, Angora, whatchamacallem."

Sally turned her head and spat forcefully in his direction.

"That can't be Sally." Tara had started to hold out her hand to the cat; she changed her mind and drew it back. "She never behaved like that."

Neville took a step backwards. Whoever she was, he didn't intend to tangle with her.

"Here we go." Tilbury ran his scanner over Sally. Salvatore reared up on his hind legs to sniff at it. "Oh, you want to try it, boy? All right, then."

Annabel hadn't realized she was holding her breath until she released it when the vet said, "No, no chip in you."

"And the other cat?" Mr. Pennyman queried.

"Oh, yes, definitely our Sally."

"But she looks nothing like—" Zenia began to protest and stopped. Sally's fur was slowly falling back into place and she looked more Sallylike with every passing moment.

"Definitely," the vet said again. "Her chip is in there."

"Oh, good," Tara said. "Now we can take her home. Where she belongs."

"I think not," Mr. Pennyman said. "I believe we'll take her with us. We wouldn't want any more . . . accidents."

"I don't know what you mean," Zenia said frostily.

"Possibly he refers to the cat in the jewel casket, the one you tried to pass off as Sally, deceased." Luther spoke in the rational detached tone of a good personal assistant explaining a difficult problem to a faintly dimwitted employer.

"That cat was dead when we found it!" Neville protested. "That's why we thought it was Sally."

"That's right," Tara agreed. "We'd never kill a cat."

"What about a human being?" Suddenly, their sanctimoniousness infuriated Annabel beyond recall. "It's too bad someone didn't feel that way about killing Arthur Arbuthnot."

Mr. Pennyman raised an eyebrow, but did not clear his throat. She was not his client.

"How dare you!" Zenia whirled to face her.

"What do you mean?" Wystan had gone pale.

"And Dora Stringer," Annabel added, with a sense of fatality. In for a penny, in for a pound.

"Are we to assume that you have some basis for these allegations?" Mr. Pennyman inquired.

"If you mean absolute proof, no." Annabel could

feel the tension dissipate in those around her and regretted that she had tipped her hand so soon.

"Proof notwithstanding"—Mr. Pennyman looked at her consideringly—"you would not, I trust, make these, er, suggestions without feeling that you had justification for them. Apart from, er, female intuition, that is?"

"How about a bloodstain on the office carpet?" Annabel was emboldened by the possibly irrational suspicion that Mr. Pennyman was on her side. Unlike the others, he appeared to be willing to consider the possibility that his late client's demise might not have been unassisted. "A bloodstain—right where Arthur Arbuthnot had been lying."

"Ridiculous!" Zenia snorted.

"I saw it, too," Kelda said.

The room went very quiet.

"There *is* a stain on the carpet," Luther agreed. "I noticed it when I was working in the office. Of course, I'm not an expert. I couldn't tell you whether it's blood or coffee. But, doubtless, someone will be able to."

"The proper testing can be arranged." Mr. Pennyman steepled his fingers again. "But is that what we really want?"

"Certainly not!" Zenia snarled. "We are not going to stand by and see our lives disrupted on the word of a drunken gin-soaked madwoman!"

Mr. Pennyman cleared his throat.

"She *does* carry a flask," Neville said. "And to work, too."

"So might you!" Annabel snapped. "If you had to deal with people like yourselves!"

"This is all so pointless—" There was a quaver in Tara's voice. "It can't be true. Who would want to murder Arthur? He wasn't a bad sort. And no one has gained by it. Except the cat."

"I think we can take it as read," Mr. Pennyman said drily, "that Sally did not stab her master in order to inherit."

A fresh shower of coins hit the main window sharply. A long crack appeared.

"Money is at the root of it," Annabel said. "Not inheritance. Just plain money. All that ready cash in the safe. I didn't take it—but someone did. Someone in this room."

"I always told Arthur he was a fool to keep that much money on the premises! It was an open invitation to burglars—and the untrustworthy!" Zenia's pointed gaze raked Mark and Luther, then turned to Annabel, just in case she thought anyone was fooled by her protestations of innocence.

"There must have been a few hundred thousand there, if one added up the value of all the various currencies," Neville said. "The woman has a point."

The others had gone very quiet. More coins hit the main window and tiny cracks began to radiate outwards from the large one. The window wasn't all that was close to breaking.

"You—" Annabel looked at Tara. "You had a lot of foreign money in your billfold on Saturday. Is the American dollar really the currency they use in Mustique?"

"Dollars are good anywhere," Tara said defiantly. "Anyway, I might go to New York next."

"Planning your getaway?" Annabel was unsurprised.

"Oh, now stop right there!" Wystan decided to intervene. "You can't think Tara had anything to do with it. If you ask me, it was"—he took a deep breath—"Dora Stringer! Yes, Dora! She was in a position of trust. She must have been quietly skimming off small sums for years."

"Certainly, Arthur was deeply concerned about something he had discovered recently," Mr. Pennyman said slowly. "That was why he made out a will in Sally's favour. It was never meant to be anything more than a temporary measure, until he got to the bottom of what was going on."

"That was my understanding," Luther concurred. "In fact, I was detailed to spread the word about the will—just in case anyone thought Arthur might be worth more to them dead than alive. But I never had time to begin letting the news leak out, as we had planned. He died so suddenly. But I find it hard to believe that Miss Stringer—"

"Dora," Wystan insisted. "Arthur caught the poor old girl in the act and she killed him and cleared the safe. Then she . . . she found she couldn't live with herself—and without him. So she—Well . . ." He trailed off, looking at them unhappily. "Not a pretty story . . . and not one we'd want to have the tabloids get hold of . . ."

"You're right, Wystan," his wife said. "This is the sort of thing one must keep in the family."

"Exactly." Wystan nodded glumly. "After all, poor Dora was practically a member of the family. Been with us all these years . . ."

"If that was the case, then a lot of money should have been found with Dora Stringer's effects," Annabel pointed out. "Was it? I think not. Whereas, I know for a fact that Tara was in possession of, literally, a bundle."

"Leave poor old Tara alone," Wystan said, with feeble gallantry "Nothing to do with her."

Tara had begun chewing on a fingernail.

"That was a truly masterly reconstruction of possible events," Mr. Pennyman conceded. "But may I suggest that, as they say, only the names have been changed to protect—in this case—the guilty?"

"Maybe Tara wouldn't mind if we searched her room," Kelda suggested. "If she's innocent, she won't have anything to hide."

"Now that is too much!" Tara surged to her feet. "Are you going to stand there and let them say things like that about me?" She looked, interestingly, to Wystan for support, before looking to Neville.

"It might not be a bad idea." Zenia had not missed that look. "I think I'll lead the search party myself."

Mr. Pennyman did not clear his throat. There was a long silence.

"I'm not going down alone," Tara warned.

"Steady on." Neville stepped forward. "No need to panic."

"Dora," Wystan insisted stubbornly. "It was all poor old Dora. One of life's tragedies—"

"Oh, shut up, you fool!" The words were Zenia's,

but the voice was Tara's. It appeared that Wystan eventually had that effect on everybody.

"Don't you call my husband a fool, you slut!" Zenia snapped.

Mr. Pennyman still did not clear his throat. He watched with as much interest as the cats, whose heads were turning from combatant to combatant.

Something heavy hit the window and the glass pane shattered, spraying glass across the room.

Any stray cat knows what it means when the rocks start flying. Salvatore took to his heels and skittered across the room for the safety of the kitchen. Sally wrenched herself free of the vet and dashed after him.

"I'll call him anything I like!" Tara's fragile composure also shattered. "Fool! Thief! *He* gave me the money. With Arthur dead, our original plan was ruined, so we were going to run away together. He'd do anything to get away from *you!* But I never thought he'd—He swore Arthur was dead when he found him. So it made sense to clear out the safe and—"

"Ah, yes." Mr. Pennyman nodded sagely. "Such an excellent reconstruction that it could have been done only by someone who was actually there. And trying to throw the blame on someone else."

"Wystan!" Zenia gasped.

Wystan, of course, Annabel realized. Who else would have been quite so inept at breaking and entering? And that sudden disconcerting flash of violence when he ripped out the entryphone wires had betrayed a side of his character usually kept well concealed beneath that weak bumbling exterior. A side that would allow him to lash out savagely at anyone who had trapped him.

"Murderer!" Tara's voice rose to a scream. "You killed Arthur! You couldn't wait until I got access to his money. You went to that safe again—and he caught you stealing. You! You killed him!" She burst into sobs.

"Erm . . . self-defence," Wystan offered. "He went for me. He was going to kill me . . . injure me. In a very nasty mood . . ." Wystan was trapped now. His face still held the neutral, faintly apologetic expression familiar to it, but his eyes moved rapidly, assessing the situation he was in, searching for a way out.

Annabel told herself that she should have suspected "Uncle" Wystan earlier. Just because a man is a buffoon, it doesn't mean he can't be a villain.

"Pennyman!" Zenia ordered. "Do something!"

"Quite right, dear lady," Mr. Pennyman murmured soothingly. "We will institute divorce proceedings in the morning."

"Never mind divorce," Zenia snapped. "I want him hanged!"

"One does understand. Unfortunately these things are never quite so simple. Apart from the fact that we no longer have the death penalty, I fear that there is insufficient evidence for the Crown Prosecution Service to mount a viable case. They don't like to undertake prosecutions without 'a realistic prospect of conviction,' as they put it."

"But he just confessed," Zenia flared. "You heard him!"

"Self-defence," Wystan said. "Self-defence, that was all I admitted. Arthur threatened me, was getting violent, went for me. I was afraid for my own life. I snatched up the letter-opener—" Wystan broke off abruptly, as though suddenly realizing that he was admitting too much.

"Mind you—" A crafty look came over his face as he decided to try to change the subject. "It wasn't just the money Arthur was upset about. I think he was beginning to suspect about me and Tara. So long as he thought she favoured Neville, he was prepared to be a bit tolerant because they were both young. But he and I were closer to the same age, so jealousy played a big part in his fury."

Not to mention outrage over the fact that Wystan was his aunt's husband. It would not be surprising, Annabel decided, if Arthur really had grown angry enough to threaten the man who was stealing his woman as well as his money.

"And I suppose Dora Stringer was trying to kill you, too?" Luther was coldly disdainful. "Not that one could blame her, if she was."

Wystan nodded slowly, as though realizing that he had just been given, however inadvertently, another out. "That's right. Poor old Dora, quite demented. You know how she was about Arthur—unhealthy, really. Got it into her head that I'd taken all that money. You know how she was—" He turned to Annabel for support. "She accused you of taking the money first."

Annabel stared him down coldly. He would get no sympathy from her.

"Ah, well . . . Dora went mad, quite mad," he said.

"Somehow she realized I'd . . . had to act in self-defence against Arthur. She went for me. I thought she was going to kill me. I was standing in front of the open window at the time—and she just flew at me. Naturally, I stepped aside to escape her. I never thought—It was an accident. You must see that."

"You can testify against him!" Zenia swung to face Tara, still trying. "You're his accomplice. They'll go lightly on you, if you turn Queen's Evidence."

"I'm no one's accomplice!" Tara drew herself up. "He duped me, just as he duped you. I have no evidence to give. I know nothing about anything. In any case"—her eyes grew shifty—"I may not even be in the country at the time of any trial."

Annabel placed a mental bet with herself that Tara already had an outward flight booked—and not necessarily to New York.

"You heard him—all of you!" Zenia looked from one to another desperately.

"Self-defence." Wystan would not now be budged.

Annabel wondered if anyone else had noticed that he was edging, almost imperceptibly, towards the door.

"I'm not going to say anything more until I have a solicitor present." He glared at Mr. Pennyman. "A good one!"

"I don't care what anyone says—" Zenia also glared at Mr. Pennyman before transferring the glare to her husband. "You'll pay for this—and it will be the first thing in all the time I've known you that you *have* paid for anything!"

"I won't stand here and be insulted any longer!"

Clutching at a precarious dignity, while moving rapidly, Wystan crossed to the door and wrenched it open, breaking into a run as he gained the main hallway.

At first, Annabel thought he had taken the wrong turning. Then she remembered the fire stairs. Wystan had good reason to know where they were located. It would not be the first time he had used them.

The others had followed her out into the hallway and were staring bemusedly at the still swinging fire door when it happened.

They heard the rush of pounding feet, the shouts, the screams—the crash. The silence.

Then they heard the solitary footsteps hesitantly mounting the stairs. The fire door opened slowly.

"I'm sorry." Cindy stood there, staring at them dazedly. "I think somebody better call an ambulance. Maybe two."

"Why?" Kelda started for the fire door.

"I wouldn't go down there," Cindy said. "It's pretty bad."

"What happened?"

"We were running up the stairs. We were almost at the top when that weedy old boy came running down, taking the stairs two or three at a time. He and Sid—Sid is a big man. When they hit bottom, he was on top. Sort of. You could do them more damage trying to untangle them. Call an ambulance and leave it to the experts."

Zenia and Tara pushed past her and rushed through the fire door. Then Zenia started screaming.

"I told her it was pretty bad," Cindy said, slumping to the floor.

"Another martini?" Annabel smiled with favour on Mr. Pennyman; he was the only one who had not asked for ice.

"I might easily be persuaded," he agreed. "You mix, as I believe they say, a mean martini, dear lady."

"I shouldn't even be in charge of a wheelchair after a couple of these," Mark said. Annabel caught Kelda's look of pleased surprise—it was obviously the first time Mark had made a joke about his situation. Things could only get better.

Mr. Tilbury took another cautious sip of his and tickled Sally's ears. She was curled up happily in his lap.

"Do you think we ought to ring the hospital and get the latest report?" Kelda asked.

"What latest? 'Resting comfortably' is all they ever say." Annabel was pragmatic—and too comfortably unwinding after the hectic day to want to get involved further. "Tara and Zenia are under sedation, with Neville standing by. Cindy has been treated for shock and is watching over Sid and all his broken bones. And Wystan—"

"I don't believe we'll have to concern ourselves with Wystan," Mr. Pennyman said. "His condition is grave—and I believe he has lost the will to live any longer." He sighed. "Even if he were to escape prosecution, his future would be bleak. I suppose it's all for the best."

"And so little Sally cops the lot." Luther shook his head bemusedly. "By default."

"Not quite," Mr. Pennyman smiled. "Arthur Arbuthnot laid careful and intricate plans, just in case. There will be a suitable redistribution of the estate in due course."

"How can you do that?" Luther was alert. "Are they going to be able to contest the will, after all?"

"The will was, shall we say, a false front, intended to be set aside in certain circumstances. I am the executor of a secret trust which Arthur set up at the same time he made the will."

"I didn't know anything about this!" Luther gulped the dregs of his martini indignantly.

"You were not intended to. That's why it was a secret trust," Mr. Pennyman smiled indulgently. "The general public doesn't realize secret trusts can exist, but they do. Their use is rare, but not unknown. They ensure that the testator's wishes can be carried out secretly, without anyone knowing. That was why Arthur set his up."

"Then the cat doesn't inherit?" Luther began to laugh immoderately. Perhaps Annabel had mixed those martinis a bit too strong. "All that fuss—and for nothing!"

"Oh, Sally will do quite well, when all is said and done. She'll live in the lap of luxury—but she won't be able to cast the deciding vote at any board of directors meetings."

"Live where?" Annabel wanted to know. "With

Zenia? Tara? Neville?" They all seemed unlikely candidates for taking the best care of her.

"Possibly, Mr. Tilbury will have that honour." Mr. Pennyman steepled his fingers at the veterinarian. "Arthur wanted to be sure Sally had the best possible care always. Mr. Tilbury is well placed to provide that, if he agrees. She will, of course, come to him with a substantial legacy of her own, enough to endow an animal hospital which, I believe, is what Arthur had in mind."

"It isn't as though Sally will be in a boarding cattery, or anything like that," Mr. Tilbury assured Annabel earnestly. "She'll live in my house, be my house cat, won't you, luv?" He rubbed her ears and Sally purred up at him. Yes, definitely a man's cat; she would be happy in his house.

One couldn't argue with that. Annabel poured another round of drinks and sank back into her chair. Salvatore sat hopefully at her feet, still slightly uneasy in the presence of someone who carried the scent of a veterinarian's surgery.

"Er, if I may ask—?" Luther looked at them. "What are you going to do about that stray? You only took him to get him out of the way before the family managed to kill him, didn't you?"

"Do?" Annabel bent and scooped Salvatore into her arms, holding him tightly. He was another good cat who had been through more bad patches than most, but not any more.

"Do?" Salvatore looked up at her, pleased and gratified as he sensed her intentions, then he relaxed against her limply, moulding himself to her contours and began to purr loudly.

"When you have an appointment for us—" She looked over to Mr. Tilbury. "I'd like to have him microchipped. After all, Salvatore is *my* cat now."

CONTINUE READING FOR AN EXCERPT
FROM MARIAN BABSON'S LATEST BOOK

TO CATCH A CAT

COMING SOON IN HARDCOVER FROM
ST. MARTIN'S MINOTAUR

Midnight.

He'd never known it could get so dark. Once you stepped away from the pale pool of light immediately beneath the street-lamp, the shadows closed in. It wasn't raining yet, but there was so much dampness in the air that it was only a matter of time. A sudden gust of wind ripped more leaves from the trees and hurled them across his path. He stumbled and nearly fell, choking back something between a curse and a sob. But he didn't know any curses vile enough and, anyway, he mustn't make any noise.

Along the side of the garage, the ground was rougher and more uneven. For a brief aching moment, he longed for the city pavements and houses huddled together in endless terraces with lights shining out of their windows, the pale blue patch of TV screens glowing inside and, at whatever hour of the day or night, music and voices.

He had never been out this late before. Alone. He was going to have to get used to it. The old life had gone. Maybe forever. He no longer trusted all the promises his mother had made. She wasn't here. Already the most important of them had been broken. She had changed her mind about the date of her return—or *he* had. They were going to prolong their honeymoon. They were going to stay away for weeks and weeks more. He was stuck here with Auntie Mags for the winter.

There was the tree, right where the gang had said it would be. It was enormous, its lower branches an uncomfortable distance from the ground, its highest branches swaying above the roof of the garage. Once he got up it, it should be easy to get onto the flat garage roof and then through the window and into the house.

Someone else's house. That was against the law. It frightened him, he had never broken the law before.

He shifted his backpack a bit so that it lay firmly between his shoulders and the straps wouldn't slip down over his arms. He hoped it was going to be big enough.

It took several jumps before he caught hold of the lowest branch and hauled himself up. He sat panting on the branch for a moment, wishing he was someplace—anyplace—else. But he had to do it. They never thought he would, that was why they had made it a condition of his joining the gang. He was going to show them. They couldn't keep him out.

How had they known he was afraid of heights? That was why they were making him do this. They thought he'd give up and go away. He'd show them!

Grimly, he pushed himself to his feet and began to pull himself upwards from branch to branch until he was on the branch that was level with the roof. He shuffled sideways along the branch, clinging to the twigs of the branch above. The end of the branch dipped beneath his weight and he clung so tightly to the twigs that he stripped them of their remaining leaves. It had to be done.

He left the shadowy safety of the tree to scramble across the open exposed space of the roof. His feet were making crunching noises. Could they hear that inside the house?

He stopped and looked at the dark window opening directly onto the roof. It belonged to an unused guest room. They told him Mrs. Nordling had plans to change it into a long French window which would open onto the roof garden she was going to create. It was a good idea, but they also said Mr. Nordling was already complaining about the expense. The general opinion was that Mr. Nordling was a cheap bastard. Maureen, Kerry's big sister, did cleaning for the Nordlings and Old Nordling was always cheating her out of the full amount due. Mrs. Nordling would try to make up for it by slipping Maureen a bit extra when she could, but she had to be careful that Mr. Nordling didn't catch her, even though it was her own money. Mr. Nordling had a rotten temper.

Kerry had it in for Mr. Nordling. That was why he wanted Robin to do this house. Two birds with one stone.

Robin flattened himself against the house—or tried to. He'd forgotten the backpack. He shrugged himself out of it and put it back on with the sack in front, then unbuckled the flap. He was going to need quick and easy access to it. Then he closed his eyes and took a few deep breaths.

He'd never even thought of breaking the law before. He was afraid of going to jail if he was caught. Now he had to break into this house and remove—steal—Mrs. Nordling's most prized possession.

No, not exactly break in. Kerry had promised him that the window would be unlocked. Maureen would see to that. It was going to be left unlocked all this week.

Maybe he could call it off for tonight and come back later in the week.

No. He'd have to go back down that tree. Once he reached the ground, he knew he would never be able to force himself back up that tree again. It was now or never. And never meant that he could never be part of the gang. And that was unthinkable, too.

He had lost his old life, his home, his friends . . . his mother. Without the gang, he was nothing.

He leaned forward, shielding his eyes, to peer through the window, to make certain it was as dark inside as it seemed. There was a sharp clink as the buckle of his backpack struck the pane and he recoiled instantly. Had anyone heard?

Darkness and silence. The Nordlings were asleep, they must be. Or—an uneasy thought came to him—perhaps they had gone out to visit friends, or to dinner and a film. Perhaps the house was empty now, but they would return at any minute. Return—and catch him in the act. The act he didn't want to think about.

He tested the window, hoping Kerry's promise was a lie. Everyone else lied. But the window glided upwards, inviting entry. He held his breath and listened again. Still silence.

He forced himself over the windowsill and stood inside, listening, waiting for his eyes to grow accustomed to the extra layers of darkness inside the house. A chill wind blew through the window behind him. He half-turned, then remembered that he mustn't close it. He might need to get out in a hurry . . . after he had found what he wanted.

No. What Kerry wanted. It wasn't going to be hurt, Kerry had assured him, but what about him? He wasn't afraid of cats. Of course, he wasn't. He just hated them. All those teeth and claws and bristling tails and yowling.

An ice-cold fatalism settled over him. He was never going to get away with this. How did you even find the cat in a great big house like this? It might be in any room. It might even be sleeping on Mrs. Nordling's bed.

Even if he found it, how could he get hold of it without being slashed to ribbons? That Leif Eriksson was one giant cat. There had been a picture in the paper of Mrs. Nordling holding him when he won a first prize in the local cat show. She almost couldn't do it. Norwegian Forest cats were about a thousand times bigger than ordinary cats and he was afr—he hated—them, too.

His reluctant feet had carried him to the door. He fished the small torch out of his sack and then the knitted gloves, which were the only ones he had. Some protection they'd be against those giant claws.

With the gloves on, he could delay no longer. He

turned the knob and the door opened smoothly with no betraying squeak from the hinges. He risked a small flash of light to get his bearings. The carpet was deep and soft, muffling footsteps. That was good. He began to close the door behind him, then stopped. How would he know which door led into the room with the open window, if he did that? He carefully pushed to door all the way back against the wall, leaving a gaping black oblong for him to dive into if he had to leave in a hurry.

All the other doors were closed. Was that a faint gleam of light along the base of the one facing the wall just at the side of the wide central staircase? He stopped and listened again: still silence. Maybe it was just a bathroom with a night-light that stayed on all night.

Where did you look to find a cat? Shading the light with his hand, he switched on the torch again and let its pale ray travel along the edge of the carpet. There was a saucer of water and a feeding bowl with a scattering of dry food beside the doorway; this was obviously one of the places the cat frequented, but it was not here now.

It could be behind any one of the closed doors. Or on the floor above, or the floor below. That was where the kitchen would be. Cats always liked to stay close to the kitchen, didn't—?

He froze. A low murmuring had begun in the room with the light on. A man's voice and then a woman's. Mr. and Mrs. Nordling weren't asleep, after all, but there was something strange about the way the voices sounded. Perhaps they were watching a television drama.

He backed away slowly, but the voices kept growing louder. Angrier. He couldn't make out the words, but they were shouting now. Both of them.

For a further forlorn moment, he clung to the hope that it was some old movie on television. Then Mrs. Nordling screamed.

The door opened and light blazed across the hallway. An object flew through the air, hit the wall with a thud and slid down it to lie motionless by the baseboard, like a fur cushion.

The door slammed shut. The shouting resumed. The screams became hysterical, the shouts inarticulate with fury.

Robin inched closer, crouched and put out his hand to touch the motionless object. It was furry and warm, but it didn't respond at all. Was it dead or just knocked out? It had hit the wall awfully hard.

Whichever, it could offer no resistance. Robin gathered it up gingerly, eased it into his backpack and buckled down the flap. Now all he had to do was get back to that open window and get out of—

"EEEEEAAAAGH! NO! DON'T! STOP—STOP—"

There was a nasty crunching sound. Even nastier than when the cat had hit the wall. Mrs. Nordling began to sob loudly. "NO . . . PLEASE . . . DON'T . . ."

"SHUT UP, BITCH! I'VE HAD ENOUGH OF YOU! YOU—AND THAT BLOODY CAT, TOO!" There were loud crashes and muffled thumps.

"MY ARM! YOU BROKE MY ARM! YOU MADMAN! I'LL—"

"YOU'LL DO NOTHING! YOU'RE FINISHED!"

Robin flinched at the sounds coming from behind that door. He might be a kid, but he knew what was going on. Should he try to do something? What could he do? He stood frozen in horror, his stomach sinking down to his ankles, his heart wrenching and lurching as though it was going to burst out of his chest—

No, it wasn't his heart. It was the cat waking up and stirring. Any second now, it would realise it was shut up in a sack and begin fighting to get free.

"YOU AND YOUR FURRY LOVER-BOY! YOU THINK MORE OF THAT CAT THAN YOU DO OF ME!"

"WHY SHOULDN'T I? HE ISN'T BETRAYING ME WITH A PROCESSION OF WHORES!"

There was a crash as some large object slammed into the door, then a thud and most of the line of light at the base of the door was blotted out. The shouts and screams became louder still and even more incoherent. There was a steady pounding squelching sound, an inaudible pleading, a choking, gurgling voice that gradually slipped into silence, although the blows went on and on until, finally, they slowed and stopped.

"Ingrid?" the man's voice, restored to sanity, called anxiously. "Ingrid? Are you all right? . . . Oh, God!"

Robin risked a quick flash of the torch at the shadow blotting out the light at the foot of the door. A dark stain seemed to be seeping into the carpet from the other side of the door. His eyes were blurred and the light was not too good, but he had a terrible feeling that it was red.

"Right . . . right . . ." There was a trace of desperation in Mr. Nordling's voice, as though, if he kept talking to his wife, he might get some response.

"Right . . . back to bed then . . ." There was a grunt and the long streak of light sprang back into place. "Bed . . . you'll feel better in the morning, Ingrid . . . Ingrid?"

"MMMRRREEEEOOOOW!" Leif Eriksson snapped back to life, even if his mistress didn't. The banshee howl sent Robin reeling across to the other side of the stairwell, clutching at the thrashing backpack.

"THAT'S IT!" There was a thud, as of a body hitting the floor. "RIGHT! YOU ASKED FOR IT! YOU'RE NEXT, ERIKSSON!"

The door was wrenched open violently, a blinding blast of light cut a swathe across the hall. Mr. Nordling lurched out of the bedroom. He was naked, dark red spolotches of blood glistening on his pale skin. His wife's blood.

Robin whimpered with a primitive terror that he instinctively knew was beyond any question of bravery or age. His hand shot up, the torch full on, blazing into Mr. Nordling's face.

"What?" Nordling flung an arm in front of his eyes. "Who is it? Who's there?"

He couldn't reach the open door leading to the open window now. Mr. Nordling was blocking his way. There was only one other way to go.

Robin launched himself down the staircase, taking the steps two at a time, slipping, stumbling, but impelled by a terror greater than anything he had ever known. Leif Eriksson wouldn't be the only one to be killed if Mr. Nordling caught up with them.

"Stop! Come back! I can explain! It isn't what you think!" Mr. Nordling was starting down the staircase now in pursuit.

The cat had stopped struggling and gone silent, probably disorientated by all the jouncing and shouting. Robin's eyes were more accustomed to the dark than Mr. Nordling's. He drew a bead on the front door and dashed for it.